DOUBLE PLAY

DOUBLE PLAY

Sara Cassidy

James Lorimer & Company Ltd., Publishers
Toronto

James Lorimer & Company Ltd., Publishers, acknowledges the support of
the Ontario Arts Council. We acknowledge the financial support of the
Government of Canada through the Canada Book Fund for our publishing
activities. We acknowledge the support of the Canada Council for the Arts,
which last year invested $24.3 million in writing and publishing throughout
Canada. We acknowledge the Government of Ontario through the Ontario
Media Development Corporation's Ontario Book Initiative.

The author makes a special thanks to the Ontario Arts Council's Writers'
Reserve Program for research and development of the manuscript.

Cover Image: iStockphoto

Library and Archives Canada Cataloguing in Publication

Cassidy, Sara
Double play / Sara Cassidy.

(Sports stories)
Issued also in electronic format.
ISBN 978-1-4594-0379-6 (bound).--ISBN 978-1-4594-0378-9 (pbk.)

I. Title. II. Series: Sports stories (Toronto, Ont.)

PS8555.A7812D69 2013 jC813'.54 C2012-908241-4

James Lorimer & Company Ltd.,   Distributed in the United States by:
Publishers   Orca Book Publishers
317 Adelaide Street West, Suite 1002   P.O. Box 468
Toronto, ON, Canada   Custer, WA USA
M5V 1P9   98240-0468
www.lorimer.ca

Printed and bound in Canada
Manufactured by Friesens Corporation in Altona, Manitoba, Canada in
February 2013.
Job # 82156

*Dedicated to the 2012 Beacon Hill Little League Major
Girls Provincial Champions*

CONTENTS

1 CHANGEUP

Finally, it's Opening Day! All the players on Juniper Bay's six baseball teams stand in line. We parade onto the diamond in our short pants, red- and blue-sleeved baseball shirts, pulled-up black socks, and scrubbed cleats. It's weird how we can be both totally excited and totally bored standing there while Island Little League president Mr. Kelsiuk drones on about "giving it your all" and "playing fair." Yeah, yeah, yeah. Then Mayor Albert Sorenson stutters nervously through a speech, his quiet words snatched up by the wind and carried off toward the graveyard south of town.

Mr. Kelsiuk hands the mayor the baseball for the ceremonial first pitch of the season. The mayor's throw is so high the catcher has to leap, his legs bent and gangly, like a toad jumping for a fly. No one laughs at the mayor's terrible pitch. They respect the ceremony too much, I guess.

Finally Mr. Kelsiuk calls, "Play ball!"

I wish we could. The boys always play first. The

stands are packed. My teammates and I kneel on the concrete at the foot of the stands, our fingers wound through the chain-link fence. We cheer on the boys we know from school, though my friends go quiet when their brothers are at bat. I don't cheer on Miles the Jerk.

The most exciting play of the game happens at the bottom of the final inning. Jake Miller is up at bat on what I call a "super full count." Not only does he have two strikes and three balls, but the team has two outs as well, so the stakes are *super* high. Whatever happens with the next pitch, things are going to move: either Jake will get a fourth ball and walk to first, making room for the next batter to start fresh, or he will strike out and the game will go into an extra inning.

But it turns out to be neither. Jake swings and misses — a strike — but the catcher misses the ball. The crowd jumps to their feet as the catcher yanks off his mask and scrambles around in the dirt. We're all screaming, "Run! Run!" Jake gets the message and takes off. But he trips halfway to first. The crowd goes "Oooh" as Jake flies through the air, then "Aaah" as he somersaults into first. His feet land on the bag, raising a cloud of dust. Meanwhile, the first baseman, who happens to be Miles the Idiot, lunges for the ball, gets it in his mitt for a nanosecond — then drops it. Jake charges to second. Miles the Ignorant makes one of his trademark weak and misguided throws, which the second baseman misses, and Jake heads to third. A few more blunders and errors, and Jake slides into home — on a dropped strike. The winning run of the game!

The team races onto the diamond, screaming and high-fiving. You'd have thought they stopped global warming or negotiated peace in Afghanistan, the way they holler and pile on each other, smudging the perfect chalk lines and trampling the rake marks that had been neat as a comb's.

But now I'm on the mound for my team, the Angels, the first girl to pitch this year. Everything feels possible. On the first day of the season, the mound is exactly regulation height, and the clay is springy and fresh. Halfway through the season, the mound will harden and shrink, but today it's a springboard. The bounce gives my pitches a little extra juice.

Across the country, most girls in Little League play softball. But ten years ago, so the story goes, when the Island Little League ordered balls for the season, there was a mix-up. Instead of three boxes each of softballs and hardballs, they got all hardballs. Correcting the order would have taken weeks and delayed the season, so it was decided that the girls in all the Island Little League towns would just go ahead and play baseball. I'm glad about that because in softball there's no mound, none at all. I love getting up on the mound, that little stage at the centre of the diamond, with everyone watching. It's like being in the spotlight, singing a solo in a musical.

I've got on my new glove. It's soft and supple and

nicely broken-in. For weeks I've rubbed shaving cream into it and slept with it under my mattress, last year's championship ball tucked inside to give it shape. When we left the house for the park this morning, I even put the glove behind one of the car's front tires and got Mom to drive back and forth over it. Phyllis was freaking out, saying the stitching would pop, but Mom had faith.

Emma Thomas approaches home plate, first at bat for the Divers. A high-pitched voice sails through the air: "Go, Ebba!" It's Emma's baby brother, Eli, who has a permanently stuffed nose. I used to babysit him, but then they stopped calling. I know why, too.

The park goes quiet. I swear, even the crows button their beaks. A cool breeze sweeps across the park, spiced with salt and the tang of seaweed. Juniper Bay is on the edge of the Pacific Ocean on the west coast of Canada. It's a town so small you can hardly fart without everyone knowing. So small that if your family doesn't look like everybody else's family, you have to hold your head high because you're going to stick out anyway. And that's what I do. I hold my head high, even when I just want to hold it in my hands and cry.

I'm the tallest in my class and on the solid side — sturdy, strong. I grew over the winter and hope my new heft will throw weight into my pitches. The band of my visor presses my thick braid uncomfortably against my head. When we're at bat and I'm back in the dugout,

I'll re-braid my hair, starting it high so it can spill over my visor instead.

Emma's in position, knees bent, head turned toward me. Her bat is held high over her left shoulder, stirring the air with little circles. She's a strong hitter, a leftie, but I'm ready for her. Only one in ten people is left-handed, but in the major leagues one in four players bat left-handed, because they have an advantage. Left-handed batters see the ball better when it leaves a right-handed pitcher's hand. So professional teams bring out a LOOGY — a Lefty One-Out GuY — who pitches left-handed to balance out the left-handed hitter. We don't have a Loogy. The best I can do is avoid pitching inside or high and slow.

"You can do it, Allie!"

Thanks, Mom.

"Strike her out!"

Thanks, Phyllis.

I can just imagine the smirks rippling through the crowd. Phyllis is mom's *girlfriend*. Juniper Bay isn't quite ready for two women living together. I mean, *really* living together. Stuffed-nose Eli and Emma's parents sure weren't. That's why they stopped calling me to babysit.

I can't think about that now. The umpire sweeps the plate one last time, tucks the hand broom into his belt pouch, then steps into position behind Kate, our catcher. Kate is crouched and waiting, glove poised in the strike zone. Sal, my best friend, is a pitcher, too. But she is playing shortstop — not that she's short. She's nearly as tall as I am and seriously lanky, with very long arms that reach out quick for balls like a frog's tongue zapping a fly. On the diamond, Sal and I have each other's backs. I take a deep breath, wind up, think *powerpowerpower.*

My pitch goes fast and straight, just the way I want. *Crack!*

A hit! I can't believe it. The ball heads straight to me — directly into my new slept-on and driven-over glove! The crowd cheers. Some people even laugh at how fast and tight the play was. My hand stings, but it's worth it. The season's first pitch is also the season's first hit and the season's first out. The scoreboard reads: 0 0 1. Zero balls, zero strikes, one out. Emma skulks back to her team's dugout.

A girl who lives on a farm outside of town, Isabelle Vogel, a homeschooler no one really knows, approaches the plate. She's even taller than me and Sal, but she squats super low so the generous strike zone between armpits and knees shrinks to nothing. Isabelle shows me her bat, holds it out toward me like a threat. Then she raises it over her shoulder.

"Out of the park, Isabelle!" shouts a man from the stands. Chances are good it's her dad.

"Go, Allie!" Mom calls, to balance him out.

I pitch. Isabelle doesn't swing. The umpire doesn't move his hands, just clicks his little counter: ball. I pitch again. Click-click: ball two. Third pitch, and click-click-click: ball three. After that fabulous first out, I do not want to walk Isabelle. But she's so squished down I can't get into her strike zone. The sun shines hard on my bare head. I can feel the part in my hair turning red, drying up like an ancient riverbed. I hate visors. Why can't girls wear full baseball caps? I've asked Coach Thor, but never got an answer that made any sense.

Concentrate.

Kate signals for a changeup. Of course! I've practised changeups all winter. There's the palmball, the circle changeup, and the knuckle changeup, but the Vulcan changeup is the best. The old time-warp special. I spread my ring and middle fingers into a V, the Star Trek salute, then work the ball into place between them. I wind up fast and, at the last second before I let go, I turn my palm downward so the ball rolls out limply from under my fingers. Looks as though the ball's going to fly — but it just kind of ambles through the air.

Isabelle starts to swing, then her face crumples in confusion. Her swing wilts, trying to time the slow ball, but no chance. Strike one! The first strike of the girls baseball season. Maybe today will be my dream game: a shutout.

I wind up for a fast pitch and throw. *Crack.* A line drive up the first-base line. Wow, can Isabelle run. By the time Annabel scoops up the grounder, Isabelle has already rounded first base. Annabel throws to Hannah on second just as Isabelle's foot touches the bag. But Isabelle over-runs the bag, lifts her foot off. She flips like a fish in mid-air and dives back for the bag, clutching at it with her fingers as Hannah tags her with the ball. It's an extremely close call — I might have called an out — but the ump lets Isabelle have it. I don't mind. I used to get worked up over close calls until I learned that umps get calls wrong twenty per cent of the time. Umpires aren't machines. They aren't robots with slow-mo playback or bionic eyesight. They're people. Lots of the time, they're ex-players, teenagers and retirees working for twenty dollars a game.

It turns out to be a slow, thick game; both teams are strong fielders. The crowd starts to dwindle, as it always does for the second game of Opening Day, the girls' game. I don't get a shutout, but the Angels end up winning 6–5. We don't leap and holler the way the boys do. We don't want the girls on the other team to feel bad. But we're happy. We high-five each other, then line up to knuckle-bump the other players — "Goodgame . . . goodgame . . . goodgame."

While I'm packing up my gear in the dugout, Hannah puts her hand over my eyes while Sal grabs my hands and pulls me out toward the diamond.

"We need you," Sal says.

I don't get it. Are they going to give me a ribbon or something? I pitched pretty well, but everyone played hard. Hannah takes her hand away from my eyes.

There's a small crowd at the mound, everyone grinning and sticking out their tongues. They start to sing.

Happy birthday to you,
Happy birthday to you!

Mom and Phyllis come out of the dugout carrying a huge cake with birthday candles that flicker in the sea salt breeze.

Happy birthday, dear Allie,
Happy birthday to you!

"I want a piece!" yells Miles the Fool. Miles is Phyllis's son, just younger than me and a total pain.

"I'll get you one once Allie's blown out the candles," Phyllis says.

I bend toward the cake, feel the warmth of the candle flames on my face, close my eyes, take a deep breath.

Whooo.

"What did you wish?" Hannah and Annabel ask right away.

I smirk and shrug. Sal smiles. She knows what I wished for: to pitch a shutout.

Mom and Phyllis hand out pieces of cake to everyone, even to the umps. But the cake isn't my usual sponge caramel birthday special. It's a peanut butter and chocolate crumb cake. Mom watches me closely as I take a first bite.

"It's Miles's favourite cake," she says nervously. "I didn't want him to feel left out."

I can't believe it. She made Miles the Whiner's

favourite cake for *my* birthday. She is always doing stuff to make sure he doesn't feel left out. What about how I feel?

"Is there more?" I hear Miles ask Phyllis.

"Sure," I say, spinning around and handing him the rest of my piece. "Here's more. Just for you."

"Thanks," he says, taking it and digging in with his wimpy plastic fork.

My heart feels like a dead ball in my chest.

2 PSTPSTPSTLESBIANS PSTPSTPST

– i hate him

I text Sal as soon as I finish my homework, which takes longer than it should because I have to ask Miles to turn down the volume on his stupid computer game sixteen times. "Get a life," he tells me. That's a joke. He's the one living in *my* house.

Sal texts back:

– and he hates you. so yr even

Sal never lets me feel sorry for myself. It's probably why she's my best friend. I mean, why would I want a friend who agrees with me all the time, especially when I'm feeling lousy? My phone buzzes again. More from Sal:

– good pitching
– u 2

– finished yr math yet?
– yeah. u?
– Vein, artery, kidney, bicep, remember?
– sigh. totally forgot. gotta go
– k. bye. oh and don't let anyone STEP on you
– he isn't my stepbrother
– not yet
– :P

Two years ago, my dad moved out. Then a year ago, Mom started dating Miles's mom, Phyllis, who lived in the next town over. One month ago, Phyllis moved in, bringing Miles with her to live in Juniper Bay. So you could say I've had three natural disasters in the last little while: an earthquake (the divorce), followed by a tsunami (mom dating a woman), followed by a flood of junk (Miles).

It was a big deal in our small town when Mom and Phyllis started dating. Not that they held hands in public or anything, but the whispers — "*pstpstpst**lesbians**pstpstpst*" — were loud. Luckily, I'd already had practice ignoring strangers' stares and the neighbours' silence after Dad headed to Las Vegas with his dental hygienist. I can still see the two of them on a tandem bicycle, Dad with his beard in a braid and his girlfriend in pink knee socks and with bright felt spikes glued all over her bicycle helmet. Oh, and Mom enthusiastically waving goodbye until they were out of sight.

I wasn't the first kid in town whose father left home. But I *am* the first kid whose mom lives with another woman. One day, in the cafeteria line, a kid turns around and tells me, "You should be ashamed of yourself."

"*You're* the one who should be ashamed," I sputtered. "Your dad wears the same track pants every day of his life. I hate to wonder what he wears when they're in the wash!"

The kid's face fell. I felt bad, but I also felt that I was on the right track; who my mother lives with shouldn't matter to anyone else, just as wearing the same pair of track pants every day shouldn't. I mean, Mom and Phyllis do pretty much exactly what my mom and dad always did. They read the paper in the morning, fight over the last cup of coffee and call out "Have a nice day" as they head off to work. Yeah, it's a little weird when they kiss each other, but it was weird when Mom and Dad kissed each other, too. Okay, it's a little weird when they share their clothes, though usually it's just their really good clothes when one of them has to go to a fancy party. They mix up their flip-flops all the time, too, but what family *doesn't* mix up flip-flops?

Mom and Phyllis have taken me a few times to the big city, to parties where there are lots of women in couples and two-mom families. Big deal. I met a kid at one of the parties. Helene is my age and we just hang out like I do with my friends at school, watching videos on our iPods, eating way too many cookies from the sweets table. We don't talk about what it's like having two moms, but we have this ease with each other, like we're sisters or something. But I think that our getting along has less to do with having two moms and more to do with having to put up with people judging our families, taking second looks or saying stupid things like "You should be ashamed."

I'm used to doing my own thing, slipping in and out of the house, hanging in my room for hours, reading or weaving. Yeah, I weave. I have a little loom and I make place mats and scarves out of jute or rags. Sometimes I do abstracts with stuff I find around town, like bits of wire and grass and plastic bags and even electrical cords. But things have changed since Phyllis moved in. She always asks, "Where are you going?" or "Where were you?" She likes to talk — a lot. "What do you think of Lady Gaga's latest song?" she'll ask. Or "Do you think Obama can be trusted?" You can't get past her without being peppered with questions. It's so bad I've started climbing out my bedroom window. Mom says it's okay if I do.

"When did you step out?" Phyllis will say when I get back from a wander around town. I'll mumble "Earlier," and Mom will just wink at me. Phyllis eventually shrugs. "Well, now that you're here, could you weigh in on whether Miles should get his hair cut?"

Mom is pretty understanding, except when it comes

to me getting along with Miles. She says I *must* get along with him. That's tough, because looking at him makes my stomach go weird like it does when I eat too much fake-buttered popcorn at the movies.

Phyllis and my mom work at the hospital. Phyllis is a psychiatric nurse, which means she helps people with mental problems. Mom's an occupational therapist, which sounds like a total yawn but is kind of cool. She helps people who have had head injuries get moving again. They joke that they're both "head nurses." Ha ha.

Actually, I should talk to that girl from the cafeteria line again. Because she was right — I *am* ashamed. I'm ashamed to be living under the same roof as smarmy, spoiled, self-centred, stinky-socks Miles.

Miles. What kind of a name is that? I was on the cross-country team for a season and ran the mile. My time was pretty good, but I needed to shave off ten seconds if I wanted to make it count. I tried and tried, but I couldn't move it. What I learned was that a mile is slow and stubborn.

And that perfectly describes Miles. Miles, who has the latest iPod Touch, new clothes from the trendiest stores, and six pairs of Vans. Miles, who gets unlimited time on the computer — *his* computer — and has to have everything I have: "She gets to go out for a sleep-over, why don't I?" "She got a cinnamon bagel!" he whines. And Phyllis says, "Aw, come here." She hugs him and runs her fingers through his greasy brown hair.

"There, there." Then she gets on the phone and rustles up a sleepover for him or goes to Bagel World and gets him not one, but half a dozen cinnamon bagels.

Once, I was going to the carnival midway during Salmon Days and he kept whining about it until Phyllis handed him a twenty-dollar bill. "Allie, you don't mind if Miles goes with you, do you?" she asked. I couldn't even answer, I was so shocked. The thing is, Miles had spent the whole day before at Salmon Days. He had even come home sick from spinning in the teacups.

Miles tells on me every chance he gets, which makes him a whiner *and* a snitch. "Allie's on her iPod instead of doing her homework." "Allie shoved her dirty dishes under the living-room chair." He leaves his dirty socks in the bathroom and toast crusts all over the house, and Mom doesn't say anything about it. I think she and Phyllis have some agreement that they will not try to parent each other's child.

There's one more person in the house. Except she's not a person. She's Patches, a skinny, old cat that Dad won in some bet when I was little. Patches is seventeen years old, which is ancient for a cat. If she was human, she'd be using a walker and eating stewed prunes. As it is, she wobbles when she walks and falls off things all the time. The other day she fell off the top of the piano onto the keys — *blang tinkle tinkle.*

The thing is, Patches is usually right beside me, snuggled against my feet in bed or curled up on my lap when I'm weaving or watching TV. When Miles moved in, she was always hissing at him. But lately she's been wandering into Miles's room and staying in there for an hour at a time. Maybe she likes the stink of his socks. I can't figure it out. But it hurts my feelings. Hurts them so bad that yesterday I snapped at Patches, then cried a little.

3 SWITCHING TEAMS

This morning Miles decides that I have the music turned up too loud. On Saturday morning the stereo is mine. As long as I'm doing my chores, I can listen to whatever I want, as loudly as I want. Today, it's Tune-Yards. The lead singer is the best thing ever.

But this morning, Miles stomps into the living room, yelling "Turn it down!" Without asking, he lowers the volume. As soon as he leaves the room, I turn it back up. This goes on for a little while, but of course he can't take it and starts yelling at me.

"Why do I have to listen to your garbage?" he asks.

I wave a toast crust in front of his face that I fished out from behind the stereo cabinet. "Why do I have to *live with* your garbage?" I ask.

"My garbage is better than your garbage," he yells.

How do I answer that? I give him a little smile that says *Really? You're pathetic.* And then the phone rings. I check the caller-id: it's Hannah. I turn down the music.

"Oh, sure. You turn it down when *you* want to turn it down," Miles sputters.

"That's right," I say. "I do."

But it's not Hannah. It's her dad, Bill Karl, who coaches practically every boys' team in town, including lacrosse, soccer, basketball, volleyball, baseball — even bowling. The guy does not look the athletic type. He's an accountant with the most amazing office in town — big leather swivel chair, big view, big desk. I saw it one day when Hannah and I were hanging around downtown after school and wanted a few dollars for Slushies. Coach Bill Karl dresses in a suit and tie and a crisp white shirt closed at the cuffs with gleaming cufflinks all the time, even on Sunday afternoon when he's in the batting cage oiling up the batting machine's pitching arm.

"Is that Allie? Dilly Dally Allie?"

"It is. But you know I don't dilly dally."

Miles starts bouncing around making faces at me, singing "*Dilly dally dilly dally Allie.*"

"I do know that," Bill Karl says. "In fact, that's why I'm calling. Allie, the Wolverines just lost their pitcher. I'm hoping you'll help out by pitching for them."

Wait, the Wolverines are a boys team. "Are you kidding?" I ask.

"Is that a yes?"

"No. It was an *are you kidding*?"

"I'm not kidding. I've seen your overhand. It's strong."

"What would be in it for me?"

"You'd be helping out your community."

"That's all?"

"And showing the world what you've got."

"I do that now, don't I?"

"Yes, but Allie, this would be a step up from the Angels. The play will be harder, faster. So fast you'd have to wear a pitchers mask."

"Those things look dorky."

"No, they look smart. They show you care about your nose and your teeth and your brain. They show that you've done the real math. That you know the chance of getting hit might be low, but the effects are catastrophic. Kids have died."

"That's cheerful."

"What'll it be, Allie?"

"Will you stop calling me Dilly Dally Allie?"

"Maybe."

"Will you tell the boys to treat me like a full team member, not some freak alien or precious weakling?"

"Yes."

I look over at Miles, who is pretending to be reading. But it's obvious he is listening — his ears are sticking out more than usual. I'd have to be on the same team as him. But I could pretty much ignore him. I'd miss my friends — Sal, Hannah, Sophia, Hazel, Sienna, all of them. But it would be cool to pitch on a boys' team.

"For one season?" I ask.

"For the season."

"Hmm."

"What'll it be, Allie?"

"I'm just not sure." I look down at Miles, who has swivelled his ball cap around — he probably thinks it will improve his hearing. Wait a minute — ball cap!

"Would I be able to wear a full ball cap," I ask Bill Karl, "instead of a wimpy visor?"

All the girls' teams wear visors. On sunny days, standing out there on the field, with nothing covering our scalps, the sun drinks all the moisture out of us. We get so thirsty. Last year Courtney the Slugger went down on her knees in the outfield from heat stroke.

"Of course. Just like the boys."

"Okay. I'll do it."

"Wonderful, Allie! You won't regret it."

As soon as I hang up, Miles asks, "What was that about?" He's trying to act as if he doesn't care, so I don't answer right away. But then, something like joy rises in me. I take a sudden big breath and my chest puffs out.

"I've been asked to play with the boys!" I blurt. "I'm pitching with the Wolverines this season."

"Big deal," Miles says, and slinks off to his room.

But the way he slams his door — *BLAM!* — tells me it *is* a big deal. For Miles, who has always wanted to be pitcher, my being asked to pitch for the Wolverines is a very big deal.

★★★

My first practice with the Wolverines is three hours after Bill Karl calls. That gives me enough time to leave a message for Mom at work. It also gives Phyllis enough time to ask me six hundred questions: Do I need a new uniform? (*D'uh!*) Am I worried about being accepted by the boys? (*Uh.*) Am I afraid? (*Um. No. Maybe nervous.*) Mom calls on her break.

"Well, dear, congratulations, I guess. Is it a move up to pitch on a boys' team?"

"Of course," I answer.

"Why?"

"The game is faster."

"But is it better?"

"Mom, it's faster and harder, and that's just better."

"Well, it will be nice for you and Miles to be on the same team."

"Oh, yeah, it will be *wonderful*. That's really why I accepted, Mom."

"Really?"

"Mom. *Seriously.*"

"Miles and Allie can carpool, Suzanne!" Phyllis shouts from across the kitchen.

"Yeah, isn't that wonderful?" I say to Mom.

"We are not going to carpool," Miles sputters.

"Yes, you are," Phyllis says. Then she yells, so Mom can hear her over the phone, "I'm trying to be strict,

Suzanne!"

"We're NOT going to car pool," Miles repeats. He stands and hitches up his brand-new plaid skater shorts. "Because we aren't going to have the same practice schedule."

"What is he saying?" Mom asks. "How can you have a different schedule if you're on the same team?"

"It's Miles talking," I say to Mom. "It's not going to make sense."

"I know what you're saying," Miles says. "But I'm not stupid, Allie. What I'm saying is . . ."

Miles pauses.

"What?" Phyllis says.

"I've got to go," Mom tells me. "Break is almost over."

"Wait, Miles has news," I say. "He's getting his thoughts in order. Do you have an hour?"

"Ha, ha," Miles says. "The reason we won't be car-pooling is that I'm not playing ball with the boys this season."

"*WHAT*?" Phyllis looks like she's going to faint. She has long believed that her butter-fingered son is going all the way to the Mets.

"But the team needs you, Miles," Phyllis says.

I bite my tongue. The team needs Miles like it needs to be exposed to ebola.

"I'm switching teams," Miles repeats. "I'm playing with the girls."

"Did you hear that, Mom?" I say into the phone. "Miles says he's playing on the girls' team."

"Oh, that's nice, dear. Listen, I've got to go. Break is over."

"Did you hear what he said? I mean, what I said he said? He wants to play on the girls' team!"

But Mom's already gone. I hang up. Phyllis is trying to reason with Miles.

"They won't let you," she says.

"Sure they will," I say, shooting a look at stupid Miles. I'm sure he has come up with this crazy idea to get back at me. "If he wears the ugly visor."

Miles's face falls. But then he straightens his shoulders and looks me in the eye.

"Then that will be the hardest part," he says. "Because it sure won't be the play."

Wow. That's real chutzpah for Miles. But he's got me confused. Is he saying girls baseball is easier than boys baseball?

Is it?

Will Miles actually be allowed to play?

And does he really hate me so much he would do something no other boy in Juniper Bay — heck, in the entire country, probably — has ever done, just to show me up?

4 THE NEW KID

"Here."

Coach Bill Karl frisbees a full baseball cap to me as soon as I walk onto the field for practice. The cap fits too loose.

"Wear it in the shower and let it dry on your head," Coach Bill Karl tells me. "It'll shrink to fit."

I wish he'd said that more quietly. The boys are grinning at each other. Small head, small brain? Mom tells me it doesn't work that way. And she knows, since brains are her specialty. Female brains have more convolutions than male brains — convolutions are the wrinkles. If you iron out the wrinkles, which would be painful, girl brains have the same surface area as boy brains. I adjust the strap to the smallest size.

"We'll have a uniform ready for you by next practice," Coach Bill Karl says. "Let me introduce you to the team."

Juniper Bay is a small town. I already know every boy on the team, minus one. Some of the boys were in my pre-school class, some are sons of my mom's friends, or the people who were her friends before she hooked up with Phyllis. There's Albert, Dad's girlfriend's nephew — he has the sticking-outest ears you've ever seen. There's Jake, the rich real estate agent's son, who made the spectacular run on Opening Day. Jake has been in my class every year since kindergarten. There's William, a math whiz and an awesome catcher. And Big Liam. He and I take piano lessons from the same teacher and even played a duet at a recital. He took up most of the piano bench, like he didn't even know I was there.

There's one kid I don't know — a tall, skinny kid. By the way he holds his glove as though it's a nest with an injured bird in it, and keeps touching his cap — pulling down on the brim, tipping it back up, taking it off, looking at it, then putting it back on — I guess he has never played ball before.

"Okay, boys, listen up," Coach Bill Karl starts. Everyone stops practising their throwing and catching and gathers around him. "This is Allie. She will be doing a lot of pitching for us this season. She's a great batter and runner, too. I want you all to welcome her to the team."

The boys shuffle about. Some look at the sky.

"You can start by saying hi," prompts the coach.

"Hi, Allie," the boys say quietly.

"With enthusiasm," Coach Bill Karl says.

The boys go quiet. A crow breaks the silence with a

throaty *click-click-click* and a caw. Coach Bill Karl squints at the boys and shakes his head.

"You know a few of the boys here already, right, Allie? Like, uh . . ." Coach Bill Karl looks around. "Miles. Where's Miles?"

"Uh," I stammer. "I have a feeling he might not be playing for the team anymore."

Coach Bill Karl moans. "I can't be short another player! Of course we've got Eric now. Has everyone met Eric? He's new to Juniper Bay. Just signed up for the team last night. How about saying hi, everyone."

The skinny kid grins shyly as the boys call out, "Hi, Eric!" They have plenty of enthusiasm for *him*. Meanwhile, I feel invisible, elbowed out, far in the outfield.

The practice is like any other practice. Coach Bill Karl hits grounders and we hustle and squat to scoop them into our gloves. Then we play a cool scrimmage game where you can only bunt. It's good practice. Even though everyone's bunting, I still manage to strike out a few players. I can't be too proud about striking out Eric, though. Poor kid can't catch, can't bat, can't throw, and has no idea where to be. He can run, though, so fast that, in the middle of the scrimmage game, Coach Bill Karl times him running the bases.

"You ever run track?" Coach Bill Karl asks, checking his stopwatch again.

"Nope," Eric answers.

"You might want to. Good news for us, anyway, because I've been wanting a pinch runner."

Eric smiles at that. But a moment later he's struggling at the plate. He swings at my pitches until I feel so sorry for him I toss an easy underhand.

"Hey!" Albert of the Big Ears says, but I shoot him a *shut-up* look.

Eric swings and misses. I send another nice slow one. Eric misses again. And another. Finally, a hit, straight to me. Eric takes off to first base — carrying the bat all the way. I could easily get him out at first but take my time throwing. Jake and the other players — except for Albert, who is scowling at me — are screaming for me to throw. They don't get that I'm doing Eric a favour. But this is my first practice with them, too, so finally, I give in. Eric's out at first. But he's smiling from making a hit, and that makes it worth it. It's a nice smile. It makes his ball cap lock into place on his head somehow, makes him look like a real ballplayer. A *cute* ballplayer. Wait a minute! Scratch the *cute*. *Focusfocusfocus*.

Later in the scrimmage, I intentionally walk Eric — out of pity, not strategy. I make sure first that he has two strikes, though, so he reaches first on a full count. He steals second really well, then makes it to third on a decent hit by Jake. Then, from third, Eric pulls off an amazing feat and makes it home on a bunt by Albert. He just smokes in while the catcher fumbles for the ball and Albert reaches first.

The New Kid

Jake gets up to bat. Big Liam is playing shortstop and I might as well be sharing infield with a grand piano. I really miss Sal. By the time Jake gets a hit, Albert has stolen around to third. Jake's hit drives up the third baseline, and I end up diving in front of Liam to get it. The ball pops off the ground into my glove before Liam has even stretched out of the ready position. I end up tagging Albert just as he starts sliding into home. And what part of his body do I tag? His butt. Everyone laughs. Except for Albert, who plasters a smile on his face. Ha, ha. When no one's looking, he shoots me a mean, *I'm-going-to-get-you-back* look. I turn to see if anyone has seen, and there's Liam, scowling at me too, thinking, I guess, that my amazing play should have been his.

5 SQUASHED HEARTS

It wasn't just the boys on my new team. Even Sal is mad at me.

- traitor
- i didn't think you'd find out B4 I could tell you
- it's Juniper Bay. news travels fast
- sorry. I only found out this pm
- found out? you didn't have a choice?
- I thought it might be cool
- cool? a bunch of boys?
- they had no pitcher. we had three. me, you, sophia.
- and i'm the best. right?
- the best in juniper bay. forgive me?
- almost
- how was practice?
- ok
- ok?
- yup
- ok. you're the best pitcher in the world. satisfied?

- your stepbrother wore a visor
- ???
- thor didn't know what to do. he let him practice but said there was no way he could be on the girls' team
- OMG
- Miles really wants to be on the team. the kid has confidence
- he just doesn't care what anyone thinks. no pride.
- he seems proud to me.
- too proud, then. gotta go. supper.
- miss you
- just supper — I'll text you soon as we're done
- no, I mean baseball
- miss you too

The house felt bigger, airier, before Miles and Phyllis moved in. Now it's crowded with strangers and their strange things. Mom says Miles and Phyllis won't always seem like strangers. But I'm running out of patience. Phyllis is nice to me, or at least tries. But Miles? Has he ever tried to get along with me?

This morning, he's slumped over his bowl, shoving Rice Krispies in his mouth, playing Jetpack Joyride on his iPod.

"Hi," I say. Mom insists that I always greet Miles.

"Huh."

Phyllis does not insist that Miles greet me.

"Any cereal left?"

Miles picks up the box, shakes it and nods. As I reach

into the cupboard for a bowl, Miles pours the rest of the cereal into his bowl. He pours in some milk. As the Rice Krispies crackle and pop in his bowl, he smirks at me. Or is it a sneer? A snirk? He holds the empty box out toward me.

"Could you recycle this?"

I don't take the box. I've learned to act like I'm not bothered. But then Patches totters out of Miles's room, down the hallway and into the kitchen. She hops right onto Miles's lap.

"Good kitty," Miles croons, rubbing Patches behind the ears so that her eyes squint and her tail straightens. I know the look. She's in heaven.

"Patches," I say. "Come here."

Patches tilts her head as if she's trying to remember who I am. I reach for her food and shake the bag. She leaps down from Miles's lap and hurries over. I pour food into her bowl and, as she eats a few bites, I scoop her into my arms. *Ugh.*

"She's smells fishy," I say.

Miles raises his eyebrows. "That's weird."

"Weird?" I say. "I think it's fishy."

"What's fishy?" Phyllis asks, coming into the kitchen.

"The cat," I say.

"The cat is fishy?" Phyllis asks. "And the fish is catty?"

"The fish died a month ago," I remind her. "Remember?"

"Of course I remember. We buried him in the front yard at the base of the ash tree. When did you get up? Have you had breakfast?"

"How could I? Miles ate the last of the cereal."

Phyllis smiles proudly. "Yes, he's a growing boy."

"He knew I wanted the last bowl."

"Surely, there's more cereal." Phyllis roots through the cupboard. "Here's some Heritage Flakes."

"Mom bought those when we were going to change our lives and start eating healthy. That was two years ago."

"I'm sure they're fine." Phyllis hands me the dusty box.

"Got him!" Miles waves his game in the air.

"Well done, honey," Phyllis says.

I head out for a bike ride, picking a handful of raspberries from the bushes in the front yard. Dad and I planted them when I was three. Suddenly, I miss Dad a lot. The berries in my hand look like squashed little hearts.

When I'm upset I usually bike down to the ocean and watch the waves come in for a while, hushing and pulsing. It's soothing. Today, after skipping stones at the ocean, I bike downtown to Sid's Sports. I lock up my bike, walk through the doors, and take a deep breath: *ahhh*. Sid's has its own aroma, a mix of leather (golf shoes, medicine balls, baseball gloves), machine oil (bike shop, workout machines), sweat (second-hand hockey gear

— *ugh*), and rubber (basketballs, Rollerblade wheels, hockey pucks). It all adds up to the wonderful stink of sport.

There's a sale in the baseball department — metal bats are twenty-five per cent off. I don't need a new bat, but I pick one up and take a strong practice swing.

"Ow!"

I whip around. A boy is moaning, doubled over. "Oh no! Did I hurt you? I didn't feel the bat hit anything — I'm so sorry!"

The guy straightens, laughing. It's Eric, the new kid. "Just playing with your mind," he says. "Hey, thanks for pitching me those easy ones last practice."

"You knew."

"Yeah, I knew. I've got a lot to learn. I've been reading up and watching videos online to try to understand the game better."

"You sure can run."

"And you sure can pitch." Eric's mouth tilts into a smile. I smile back, trying to make my smile small and cool, but a giant grin keeps breaking my face open.

I help Eric pick out a baseball glove — he was using a crappy vinyl thing at practice and Coach Bill Karl told him it was unsafe. I show him how a glove should fit, how it has to stop at the top of his wrist so the heel of your hand sticks out and your hand can move freely. I tell him how to soften the leather with shaving cream and how he should sleep with it between his mattresses.

We test it out with a ball from a sale bin, playing a game of catch in the aisle. Eric tells me his family has moved to town for a year. His mother is a biologist and has a research contract to study some slug that's endangered. I can't imagine why anyone would care that much about a slug.

"Slugs are the original composters," Eric says. "If it wasn't for them, the forests would be small and dull. Slugs work like crazy. They eat the junk on the forest floor and turn it into dirt. They also spread seeds and spores by eating them and —"

"So, forests are made of slug poo."

"Pretty much," Eric says, his mouth tilting into that grin again. Eric says that his mom looks for taildropper slugs nonstop, goes around poking at piles of leaves and rotting logs. She hasn't found any yet in Juniper Bay. I tell him that if I wasn't finding any, I'd stop believing there were any and just choose something else to study. But Eric says that's what makes his mom good at her job.

"She believes in the possibility of the taildropper," he says. "She *hopes* it's in the area. She has faith. It's almost like she brings the species back to life by looking so hard, by not letting them be dead . . . not yet."

We throw the ball back and forth.

"I heard some guy is trying to get on the girls' baseball team," Eric says after a few throws.

I stiffen. "That's right."

"But boys aren't allowed on girls' teams, right?"

"I don't think so," I say. I'm biting my tongue so I don't rant about what a huge jerk Miles is.

"You don't seem too happy about it," Eric says.

"How can you tell?"

Eric laughs. "By the way you're chewing your lip and glaring and — *ow* — throwing harder."

"The guy's just doing it just to get attention."

"Well, it is kind of weird that you can play on a boys' team, but a boy can't play on a girls' team."

A woman in tennis whites comes out from behind a rack of sweatbands. "It's a double standard," she says. She's holding a racket that looks as though it broke in the middle of a game and she hustled to Sid's for a replacement. "Sorry to eavesdrop, but it *is* the talk of the town."

An old man trying out a weightlifting bench puts in his two cents. "The boy must be some kind of sissy."

"Why would playing with girls make you a sissy?" I ask. "I play with girls all the time, and I'm not a sissy. Anyway, this boy is *not* a sissy."

I don't know why I say that. Why am I defending Miles?

"He's in it to meet girls," chimes in a middle-aged man with longish hair looking through a rack of work-out pants. "That's why I go to yoga. To meet women."

"I heard the kid is meeting with the president of the Island Little League today," calls out a clerk from over in the skate department. "To plead his case, you know?"

I didn't know that. I can just imagine Miles whining to Mr. Kelsiuk about how unfair everything is. Just like at home.

"There's something about his family," the old man says. "I can't remember what it is. Something — corrupt."

My heart lurches. I chuck the baseball back into the sale bin and head out of the store. I feel like I might be sick.

"Hey!" I hear Eric call. "Wait up!"

The door closes behind me and I'm out on the street. The day is alive with construction sounds, seagulls swooping in the ocean air, and tingly spring sunshine. I take some deep breaths until I feel calmer. I unlock my bicycle from the *No Parking* sign, but when I try to pull it away, it won't move. Someone has locked their bike to mine. Great. Just when I wanted to make a quick getaway.

Eric bursts out of Sid's with a shopping bag in his hand. "Why did you leave so fast?"

"I needed air."

Eric looks at the bike locked to mine.

"I know," I say, kicking the bike. "Some stupid idiot locked his bike to my bike."

Eric smiles. "That stupid idiot was me."

"Oh."

"Sorry. I'm a bit of a klutz."

Eric looks at me. I look back at him. And it's like

our eyes lock up together, just like our bikes. He smiles. I smile. Then I get another wave of nausea — sweet nausea this time, churned-up happiness.

"See you at practice?" Eric asks, detaching his bike from mine.

"See you at practice," I manage to answer.

6 LIKE A GIRL

The house is empty when I get home. Phyllis has left a note on the black dresser in the front hall:

How was your afternoon? Where were you? Have you eaten? Are you tired? Have you been drinking water? Hot day, hey? Do you like the new paint colour on the front door?

Meow.

I follow Patches's muffled voice to Miles's room. I press my ear up against his door. She's in there. I push on the door. The room is dark and stuffy. I open the curtains so that I can see, then a window so that I can breathe. There's clutter everywhere — dishes, clothes, computer cords, and game cases all over the floor.

Meow.

I follow my old cat's cries to Miles's dresser. Miles must have accidentally closed her up in a drawer while she was asleep in there. I've done that, too. I open the top drawer: no Patches. Middle drawer: no Patches.

Bottom drawer: Patches! She leaps into my arms. But whoa — what is that stink? I feel around in the drawer, shove T-shirts out of the way. There's a pile of greasy empty sardine tins under a black sweatshirt. So it wasn't just Miles's socks that were smelling up the place.

"Oh, Patches," I say, rocking my golden-haired cat to calm her. "He's bribing you with sardines. He's using you to get to me."

I carry Patches into my room and close the door. Then I dig out her old toys from the back of my closet. When we first got Patches, I played with her all the time. I guess somewhere along the line I fell out of the habit. As we play, I realize that Patches doesn't have as much energy as she used to. She falls asleep on my lap, her weight heavy and warm. I work on my latest weaving project — a placemat with telephone wire and zap straps.

"I love you," I whisper into the soft triangle of Patches's ear. "I always have loved you, and I always will love you. Love lasts longer than sardines."

★★★

Around suppertime, Miles and Phyllis clomp into the house.

"He wasn't even listening!" Miles complains. "He just played with his tie and said the same thing over and over: '*Boys cannot play on girls' teams. That's Little League policy.*'"

"Do you need a snack, dear?" Phyllis asks.

"No! I don't need a snack!" Miles yells. "Stop asking me. I'm writing a letter to the newspaper right now. Hey! Who was in my room? Who opened the curtains and went through my stuff?"

"Now, why would someone have gone into your room?" Phyllis says. "Here's a plate of apple slices."

"I DON'T WANT APPLE SLICES!" Miles slams his bedroom door so hard the whole house shakes. My headboard shudders against the wall. Patches stirs in her sleep.

Phyllis knocks at my door. "Would you like some apple slices, Allie?"

"Sure, Phyllis. Thanks."

★★★

After supper, I sneak out of my bedroom window, hop on my bike and pedal to practice. My sports bag slides off my shoulder a few times, making me veer into traffic, but I make it to the park in one piece.

"Our first game is tomorrow," Coach Bill Karl announces, handing out the season's game schedule. "We play Cedar Grove."

Cedar Grove is the next town over. It's where Miles lived before moving to Juniper Bay.

"I watched them practise last night and they're strong hitters. Our fielding has to be top notch. They were hitting lots of fly balls from what I saw, which is lucky for us. We'll practice catching flies tonight, and also refresh our covers at second base. Yes, Eric?"

"Uh, did they know you were watching their practice?"

"I don't really care if they knew or not. I got wind of the practice, drove over to Cedar Grove, parked the car and watched."

"With binoculars?"

"Monocular."

Eric looks around nervously. "Is someone watching *us*?"

Coach Bill Karl shrugs. "Don't know. Welcome to the big leagues. Which reminds me, you're all getting matching team bags this year. It'll make us look sharp, like we've got our act together. It'll psych out the other team. Also, we'll meet in the school yard behind the ballpark before the game and walk into the park together. That's also intimidating. And when you do your warm-up throws, do them in sync. Got it?"

The guys yell, "Yeah!"

Except Eric. He bites his lip, then raises his hand.

"Is all that going to make us play any better?" he asks. "I mean, we're just faking them out."

"Psychology," Bill Karl says, tapping his finger to his head. "Get the upper hand in the battle of wits and you *feel* more confident. When you're confident, you have nothing to worry about; your mind doesn't skitter ahead of your body. It can relax and let your body do its thing."

I've been trying to blend in with the players on the Wolverines, trying not to stick out like a sore thumb. I try to do what the boys do, move the way they do and stay quiet. I don't understand what they're talking about half the time — clips they've watched at each other's houses, new apps, other boys at school. Albert has scowled at me ever since I tagged him out via his behind, and Liam glares at me after I caught that fly. But for the most part, other than Eric, everyone pretty much just ignores me. I can only hope that my pitching will win their respect.

The pitching mask feels totally weird at first. It's this big plastic cage halfway up my face that I have to look over and through — that I have to look *past*. I feel like a dog in one of those post-surgery collars. Or like a robot — no, a cyborg. I get used to it pretty quickly, though. If I start to think about how much of a dork I look in it, I just call up a mental picture of my nose smashed into a million bloody pieces. That would be worse. So I play it cool, focus on my pitches.

But today I blow it completely. I rack up enemy after enemy after enemy. First, one of my pitches hits the ground just past the plate and sprays dirt in Jake's face through his catcher's mask. Coach Bill Karl rinses Jake's eyes in the dugout, but it looks like he might have a scratched cornea. Then, just as Jake's mom arrives to take her son to the clinic, one of my pitches hits Francis full in the face. In a flash, his cheek bruises the blue-green colour of Matheson's Pond, murky at the height of summer.

"I'm so sorry," I call to Jake as his mom leads him to the car. One of his hands is held over his injured eye but he's able to roll his other eye at me.

"I'm sorry," I call to Francis, who moans "*Ow, ow, ow*" as he cradles his bruised cheek in his hand. He looks over at me and moans louder.

I feel helpless watching the car drive away. Eric tries to give me one of his tilty smiles, but it doesn't help.

The last hit of the scrimmage flies high, right over the diamond, and Big Liam and I both run for it.

"Mine," I say. I back up and make a perfect catch. I feel that satisfying smack as the ball sockets into the glove. A runner is halfway between third and home so I haul my arm back to throw to third for an awesome double play, and my elbow bashes Big Liam in the mouth. There is blood everywhere, dripping onto the diamond in dark red dots and smeared across Big Liam's top lip. Coach Bill Karl hustles over to Big Liam. But he doesn't put his arm around him, the way Thor does when an Angels player is hurt. He just touches him quickly on the shoulder and asks, "You all right, buddy?"

"He shouldn't have been so close," I croak. "I called that pop, but he kept crowding me."

"I never heard you call it," Coach Bill Karl says. He looks me in the eye. "You need to speak up, Allie."

"I'm sorry," I tell Big Liam, who has taken off his shirt and is holding it to his nose. He won't even look at me. Out of the corner of his mouth, he hisses, "You'd better stop throwing like a girl."

"Wh–what?" I sputter.

"You heard me," he says, and spits blood at the ground.

Coach Bill Karl doesn't seem to notice that I feel lousy about hitting Jake, Big Liam, and Francis. If it were the Angels, Coach Thor would have tended to me, too, not just to the injured players. I want to know that someone understands how sorry I am.

7 SISTERHOOD

My cellphone buzzes. I open my eyes. The morning sunlight stings like lemon juice in my eyes.

- wakey wakey
- why so early, Sal?
- check out the Juniper Bay Times. your brother wrote a letter to the editor. page 4
- he is NOT MY BROTHER
- right

I elbow Miles out of the way as he reaches for the paper on the breakfast table.

"That's mine!" he says.

"No, it's not," I say. "It's mine. This is my house, Miles. Just like Patches is my cat."

Miles wrinkles his face and pretends he's about to cry. He even sniffs a few times and his eyes redden. Did he take acting classes?

"I live here," he finally says. Then, as if he isn't

quite sure, he adds, "I do."

Then — victory — he heads back to his dark bedroom.

The floor is still cool under my bare feet, but the room is already warming with the spring sun. I shake open the newspaper and turn to page 4:

Boy Wants to Play With Girls

Dear Editor,

I'm an 11-year old boy who has played Little League baseball for six years. I want to play on a girls' team this year but the League president says boys can't play on girls' teams. But girls can play on boys' teams! It's a double standard. It's discrimination. I hope your newspaper can support me in my cause.

Yours,
Miles Kowalchuk

I knock at Miles's bedroom door.

"Big words," I say. "Dis-crim-in-a-tion. Five syllables."

"Shut up," Miles squeaks.

"Touchy touchy."

"SHUT UP!"

"Miles!" Phyllis comes out of the bathroom, twisting a towel around her wet hair.

I put the newspaper in her hands. "Check out his letter," I say.

"Is this what you are fighting about? And why are you out of bed so early on a Saturday, Allie? Does that nightgown need a mend? Do you think I should colour my hair?"

"Page four," I say. I escape to my bedroom to text Sal.

- *what a jerk*
- *he's a good player*
- *r u kidding me?*
- *he can read the batter. he gets himself into the right spot to catch the ball*
- *but then he misses it*
- *he's getting better*
- *he only joined the Angels to get at me for playing for the Wolverines*
- *he shakes things. he takes on Thor about his rules, like why we can't eat in the dugout. he even came up with a better series of catcher's signals and thor accepted them. maybe he just wants to play girls ball*
- *why would he want to do that?*
- *you used to want to play girls ball.*
- *that's different*
- *do you miss us even a little?*
- *um*
- *what does um mean?*

How can I explain to Sal that the *um* means *ouch* and *wow* at the same time. I miss the Angels a lot, that's part of the *ouch*. The *ouch* is also not fitting in with the Wolverines, the lonely feeling of being stuck in a parallel world where I don't belong. A world where no one talks to me or forgives me for simple baseball errors, and no one cheers even when I strike three players out in a row.

And the *wow*? That's from getting stronger. I'm stronger at bats and in the field now. Coach Bill Karl and the boys just expect me to be trying and getting better on my own. I miss Coach Thor and the girls supporting and helping each other. But a thought stirs in my mind — maybe I can do it by myself. As they say, diamonds come from pressure. But who's to say the pressure won't just squash me flat?

- um means i miss you, and I'm learning a lot
- so it's bad and good
- yup

Saturday mornings after Dad left, Mom would make a big tofu scramble, which sounds disgusting but is delicious, like chewy scrambled eggs. Then, she and I would bike to the park for a game of bocce. But since Phyllis and Miles moved in, Mom hardly ever makes tofu scramble. I know she tries to balance her time between me and Phyllis, but it's like Phyllis gets her now, and she's just my mom again, not my friend, too.

Today is a no-tofu-scramble Saturday. Phyllis and

Mom are in the kitchen, coming as close to arguing as the lovey-doves ever do.

"Sweetheart, girls can play on boys' teams. Miles just wants to know why it doesn't work the other way around," Phyllis says.

"Yes, but, honey, why is Miles the only boy to ever want to play on a girls' team? What is driving him? It has something to do with Allie, I know it."

"You mean, darling, that he's being mean-spirited?"

"No, no. Just, maybe, competitive, dear."

"He just wants things to be fair, sweetness."

"I have never seen him as a crusader for gender rights before, love."

"Are you saying, dear heart, that because he's a boy, he can't stand up for sisterhood?"

And on and on. They don't even notice me. I grab a granola bar and juice box and sneak out again.

Patches is meowing as though she's in trouble again. I knock at Miles's bedroom door but there's no answer. I push the door open. I shouldn't snoop, but I can't help noticing his computer is open to a web page: Differences Between Girls and Boys in Sports. It draws me in. The article says boys are stronger and faster than girls, and have quicker reflexes. But boys and girls are equally competitive. And girls can play a more complex game, with better teamwork and more complicated plays. Their focus isn't just on scoring. Girls have better flexibility and often better endurance, but they are generally more physically cautious than boys. The article says at the end that it isn't about who is a better athlete, but rather which sports are better suited to which gender.

As I read, Patches noses my ankles and rubs her cheek against my leg. I reach down and stroke her. But what's this? She's on some kind of leash. A grey piece of string is tied to her collar at one end and to Miles's bedstead at the other. Looking at it, I feel choked, too. I feel separated from Patches, as though I've let her down. I unknot the leash and press her close. But she keeps trying to pull away. She gets loose and bounds onto Miles's dresser where she starts pawing at a plastic bag from Gemma's Grocery.

The bag is full of tins of sardines. A receipt lists ten cans totalling $8.90. Miles doesn't have a job, and his allowance is the same as mine — five dollars a week. Where on earth does he get the money to buy Patches so much fish?

"Patches," I say. "I went with Dad to pick you up after he won you in that bet. You lived in a shabby old house on the edge of town with four other cats, your brothers and sisters. I didn't want to tear you from your siblings, but Mom said your owner wasn't able to look after you. I didn't have any sisters or brothers myself — I still don't, definitely not that stinky Miles. And I thought, well, I could be your sister and you could be mine."

Patches watches me as I speak but as soon as I take a breath, she paws the bag.

"Listen, Patches. I can play Miles's game, too. Only I would never put you on a leash. Now I have to re-train you. Remind you who is your sister, who dangles cat toys for you and changes your water and lets you in and out of the house at all hours."

Something gnaws at me. Why do I feel like I'm lying? It's the space of time that I'm ignoring, the last few years when I haven't been playing with Patches as much, and haven't been good about changing her water or letting her into the house. Mom must have taken over those jobs at some point, and I didn't notice.

A breeze flows through the room and I realize that Miles's window is open. I haven't seen Miles all morning. Is he climbing out his window the same way I do? Is he sneaking around, too?

Patches leaps onto Miles's bed and stretches across the pillow. I watch her settle in, see how comfortable she looks. Then I notice something fuzzy sticking out from under the pillow. It's an old teddy bear, with floppy ears and fuzz worn thin on its belly and legs. I grab the bear and it sags in my hand. I guess that stupid, snivelling Miles has loved this stuffy for years. Still loves it, probably. Maybe he even cuddles it at night, whines to it about his awful *stepsister*.

I tie the grey string around the teddy bear's neck. I choke that bear on the ugly old leash. See how that feels, Miles the Meanie.

Then I pocket a tin of sardines from the shopping bag, take Patches into my arms and head to my room, grabbing the can opener from the kitchen on the way. Patches eats every last bit of the fish, including the blank-eyed heads and the silvery tails. Then she noisily chases the tin across the floor, licking the last of the oil from its corners. She falls asleep in my lap as I weave a new mat for her cat bed. It will replace the worn-out one I made for her years ago when she was new to the house. I am determined to look after Patches, to be the best sister that a cat ever had.

8 BOYS DON'T SING

"Good eye!"

"Now you know what the good ones look like!"

"Great cut!"

"Protect the plate!"

"Way to get a piece of it!"

"Great swing, just wasn't your pitch!"

"Look alive, Wolverines!"

"Swing at the good ones!"

"That's the way to stay in the battle!"

We look cool coming onto the field, with matching sports bags and streaks of zinc oxide under our eyes like war paint. But Jake has a patch over his eye because his cornea did get scratched, which means he's on the bench for the game.

"I need both eyes for depth perception," he tells me, adding sarcastically, "It's just a little important to know where the ball is."

Francis's cheek looks like a squashed plum and Big Liam's lip is swollen, but at least they're able to play.

I guess Coach Bill Karl wants to show them he's on their side, because he doesn't let me pitch until the fifth inning. Meanwhile, the other pitchers get zero speed. They throw so many balls, the parents in the crowd stop yelling the encouraging "Good eye!" The other team gets five forced runs, just from the bases being loaded with walks. We are losing 9–0 when Coach Bill Karl finally lets me pitch.

"You can do it, Allie," Phyllis yells from the stands. "Catch us up!"

I look at her and raise my right eyebrow: *Really?* The crowd laughs. But I do manage to shut down the other team. Three strikeouts in a row that inning. I look at Coach Bill Karl as if to say, "Now, do you remember why you asked me to pitch?" He doesn't smile or nod or anything.

I feel hollowed out with missing the Angels. We always joke and tease each other. Coach Thor even lets us tease him. We don't take the game so seriously. No, that's not right. We take the game seriously. We play our hardest, for sure. We just don't take *ourselves* so seriously.

We are at bat. The Rangers pitcher has a crazy routine before he throws, starting with tapping on his ball cap visor with his non-throwing arm, then wagging his head side-to-side, glancing at second base, glancing at first, a sneer, lifting his left knee up, leaning 45 degrees forward, leaning backward, drawing his arm back, and — with a deep grunt — finally, the pitch.

In response, Eric plays up his own routine. He chucks his bat from one hand to the other, one-two-three times, then taps the plate with gusto. Then he wiggles his hips widely as he gets into place to swing. After all that, he gets three balls and two fouls. Then, on a full count, he swings at a high pitch. It's the kind of swing that makes you groan — like he's swatting at an insect in the air or casting a fishing rod. But he gets a hit! The low ball skims the shortstop's legs and grounds into the right outfield. By the time the outfielder gets the ball to infield again, Eric has run a triple. The boys cheer like mad from the dugout.

My turn at bat. I have my own home-plate routine. I grip the bat at the very end and swing it around twice. Then I pound the plate once with the end of the bat, raise it to shoulder level, straighten my index fingers to make sure my hands are aligned on the grip — Sal taught me that trick — lift the bat over my shoulder, and get my feet shoulder-width apart and solid on the ground, knees bent in a loose squat. I stare the pitcher in the eye, taunt him. *Send me your toughest*, I say with my eyes. *Send me your worst.*

The first pitch is inside. I jump out of the way, careful not to swing. Ball one. The second pitch is outside. I know it is. I don't swing, but the ump calls a strike. The third is a perfect pitch for a batter — right in the strike zone, directly over the plate. Something wonderful happens for me when there's a perfect pitch. The whole world goes slow-mo.

I glance at the sweet spot on my bat and it's throbbing like a hot spot. I've seen it a hundred times while lying in my bed, that spot on the bat that will send the ball over the fence, all the way to Matheson's Pond. Mom teaches her patients to visualize. If, after a head injury, someone is having trouble holding a cup or walking up stairs, Mom tells them to imagine doing it over and over in their mind, to imagine the feel of the cup's handle in their fingers, or feel their knees lift as they walk. I lie in bed and imagine my bat meeting the ball right at the sweet spot. I imagine power rising up through the ground of the batter's box, into my feet, up through my legs and hips, through my back and arms and into my swing.

CRACK. Yes!

I'm halfway to first when I gather from the cheering of the crowd that Eric has slid home. My foot lands on the first-base bag — *poof* — just as the first baseman catches the ball from outfield. *Poof, smack*, in that order I beat the ball. The umpire's arms wave low, palms down. Safe!

Phyllis and Mom are screaming in the crowd. I look up at the scoreboard just as the number of runs ticks, finally, from 0 to 1. I look over at the dugout, but no one's really cheering. Big Liam openly grimaces at me. I feel the sting. I get this picture in my head of Sal and Kate and Sophia and Hannah in the dugout, jumping up and down and screaming their loudest. That's what they do. They pour energy into every good play. They also sing through our games: *Hey, batter, batter, swing!* Or *Allie, Allie, that's her name. She's the reason we're gonna win this game!*

The boys don't sing. Ever.

I look for Eric. He's still out of breath from running into home, his smile wide. Come to think of it, he's the only boy on the team who actually smiles when he gets a run, who actually celebrates. The others are too cool to show their excitement or too focused on the next great thing they can do. It's like every move they make is part of a scheme, just one stage in a plan — for what? Where are they trying to get to?

I suddenly worry that Eric will stop smiling at some point, that he'll learn to control the muscles in his face even when he's bursting inside. Do the rest of the boys still burst inside even when they don't smile? If they train their faces not to show their feelings, then why not just stop having feelings at all?

Big Liam's fly ball ends the inning. The Rangers' second baseman catches the pop and tosses the ball to first well before Big Liam gets there. The Rangers drop their fielding stance. They lower their gloves, straighten their knees, droop at the shoulders. The pitcher drops the ball to the mound and everyone leaves the diamond. It's like they shrug off the entire inning.

I always look at the diamond between innings, how

it seems to be resting, waiting, even taunting — it wants its players back. The diamond is nothing without us, just a field. If I stare too long, I can imagine crickets in the grass, worms digging through the dirt, ants busy in their tunnels. During the winter, between ball seasons, I avoid looking at the diamond when we drive past. It looks unkempt and slobby, decaying in hibernation.

Now, though, I reach for my pitching mask, which I'm getting used to. I head up to the mound to practise a few pitches with Jake, remembering to duck every third pitch so he can throw to Big Liam at second, over my head, so he can out some imaginary steal. We move like clockwork, build up a rhythm, massage the diamond out of its short slumber. I even stomp my feet on the mound a few times as if to say. "Be wakeful, hold me up, keep this game airborne."

"Play ball," the umpire finally shouts, and the sixth and final inning is launched.

9 LIES AND LONELINESS

A League of His Own? Local Boy Forbidden to Play Ball with the Girls

Feature Article by Kelsey Durns

Local boy Miles Kowalchuk says he isn't trying to make a joke or stir up trouble. The Little League baseball player's reasons for wanting to play on a girls' team are simple.

"I just want to," said the boy in an exclusive interview with the *Juniper Bay Times* yesterday. "Girls get to play on boys' teams. Why shouldn't it work the other way?"

Miles has been practising with the local girls' team the Angels for two weeks, but Little League executive Thomas Kelsiuk says he is not welcome to play in games.

"It is against the rules," League President Kelsiuk told the Times as he fumbled in his desk for the League Charter. When asked why, he said that the boys' level of play may intimidate his new teammates. He added that a boy would also distract the girls from their game.

Lies and Loneliness

The Times attended a recent Angels practice. Miles looked to be playing at the same level as the girls. The girls have apparently accepted him.

"He's okay," said Annabel Corporal, the Angels first baseman. "I don't really notice that he's a boy anymore. Well, I notice, but, you know, he fits in."

Teammate Sal Jaffna was equally positive "He has a great eye for where a batter is going to send a ball. He's nice, too."

The *Times* contacted the National Little League office in the capital.

"We want girls to play ball. It's fun and healthy," said National Little League President Tom Nanoo. "When the little league began, a few girls signed up, but after T-ball and mini-minor, the game got rougher and, I have to say, the culture in the dugout got cruder. Girls quit playing ball.

"We came up with the solution of girls-only teams. It works. Girls can be with their friends and play the way they want to play."

Angels coach Thor Danielson has allowed Miles to attend Angels practices, but Miles sat on the bench through the first three games of the season.

"It's hard," Miles confessed. "The bench gets pretty hard after a few innings of sitting. But it's also hard to watch a bunch of kids play and not be able to join them."

The Little League will vote in a closed meeting this evening on whether Miles Kowalchuk will be allowed whether Miles will be able to play ball the way he wants it. *The Juniper Bay Times* will report their decision tomorrow.

★★★

Everyone is talking like crazy at practice. But when I approach, it's like someone presses the mute button. Of course they're talking about Miles's campaign to be on the Angels. From what I can tell, they aren't on his side. I drop my bag and sit at the end of the bench. There's still ten minutes before practice starts, so I get out my iPod. As soon as I clamp my headphones to my ears, the chatter starts up again. I stare across the diamond at the scoreboard. One of the field custodians is up on a ladder replacing the lightbulb that counts the second strike.

Someone bumps my knee. It's Big Liam. He's asking me something. Everyone is watching. I lift one of the earphones off my ear.

"I said, 'What are you listening to?'" Big Liam says. "Mother Mother?"

Several of the boys snicker. I freeze. Embarrassment prickles my skin. Mother Mother happens to be one of my favourite bands right now — everyone on the west coast is listening to them. But Liam is just trying to poke fun at me.

"I guess Miles is getting a little confused," Big Liam says, "about whether he's a boy or a girl." "That's stupid," I say.

"You saying I'm stupid?"

I don't answer.

"What's going on here?" Coach Bill Karl enters the dugout. He looks at Big Liam towering over me. Then he looks at me and his face falls. He looks sad, defeated. He shakes his head.

"Everybody out on the field," he says. "Except Allie."

Great, more attention. I can't help widening my eyes at Coach Bill Karl as if to say *shut up*.

"I need to go over pitching strategy with her," Coach Bill Karl tells the others, saving himself, saving me. "She's our best pitcher, after all."

"Oooh," say a few of the players. They realize that he's taking a dig at Big Liam, who keeps begging Bill Karl to let him pitch more.

As soon as the team is out throwing and catching, Bill Karl sits on the bench beside me.

"You don't even have to tell me what they were saying," he says. "I know."

"You do?"

"I do. I want to tell you something."

Coach Bill Karl takes a deep breath, puffs out his cheeks, lets the air out slowly, then begins.

"My mom lived with a woman when I was growing up — in this same town. They told everyone they were cousins. They even told me that. When I figured things out, they made me keep up the lie. I would tell everyone that Mandy was my second cousin. My mom and Mandy loved each other. For forty years, they really talked and listened to each other in a way I've never seen people talk since. They were always in the middle of a conversation about something, about anything, about everything. And, sure, they slept in the same bed.

"Both died a few years ago, just a few months apart. They're in Juniper Bay Cemetery. A beautiful place. But you know what? Their graves are four rows apart. They weren't brave enough to buy one plot and a double headstone. And I didn't feel that I could ask for one, even after they were dead. I had to honour them by carrying on the lie."

"That's awful," I say.

"Yep. A whole life of lying. By the way, the two of them were ballplayers when they were girls. They played Little League."

I can't say the boys are any nicer for the rest of practice, just more careful. I guess Miles's move to be on a girls' team makes them nervous. But why do they swipe at *me* because they feel uncomfortable?

Eric tries to talk to me a few times. He's confused about why the boys are being mean. He doesn't get it, because he doesn't know about Mom and Phyllis. And I don't want to explain it to him. For the first time ever, I'm watching the clock during a baseball practice. For the first time ever, I'm relieved when practice is over.

It's a Thursday evening, a plain, totally neutral time

of the week. Thursday evening is a free square, a blank page, an empty room. It doesn't promise anything, so it can't disappoint you, which is nice. Nothing much happens on a Thursday evening, but I guess that means anything could.

This Thursday evening is warm. As I bike home from practice, the sun is just setting. Downtown is quiet. The shops are closing up. An armoured truck pulls away from the bank with the day's deposits. The barber sweeps up the hair from the barbershop floor. As I pedal past the lane behind the barbershop, I hear a loud clang. Someone is lifting the lids of the garbage cans and peering inside. I've seen people do that in the city, looking for uneaten food or recyclables, but in Juniper Bay?

This person is short, with their hood of the hoodie pulled high, so it's hard to tell if it's a boy or a girl, or a scrawny man, or what. The person pulls out a pop can, shakes the last drips out onto the ground and lowers it into a backpack.

I know that backpack. I recognize the person's movements, the slowness.

It's Miles.

He swings the pack over one shoulder and walks to a dumpster further up the lane. He climbs up on its big square handle and looks over the top. He hoists himself higher and leans right in. As he hangs there, halfway in the dumpster, a cat dashes out from between two buildings, crosses the lane and jumps a fence. I think of Patches and suddenly I know what Miles is doing. He collects bottles and cans to cash in. It's how he makes the money to buy all those tins of sardines. This must be where he goes when he sneaks out his bedroom window.

I would find it pathetic and stupid, except for one thing, a gesture that burns into my mind so that all the way home I blink my eyes and shake my head to try to get rid of it. It's how Miles looks when he slings his backpack over his shoulder and moves on to the next garbage can, his head lowered and his shoulders slumped. He looks sad and resigned, sure. But worse than that, he looks lonely. Very, very alone.

10 NO SCORE

Friday evening the Wolverines play a team from Long Lake. It's been raining all afternoon and a light drizzle still falls, but a blue evening sky is coming our way from the east, eating up the clouds. Coach Bill Karl hands out buckets of Diamond Dry — ground-up corn cobs that soak up puddles — for us to spread on the field's soggy spots.

Francis no longer wears an eye patch. When we meet in the parking lot with our matching bags and get in formation to walk onto the diamond as one team, Francis points at his two free eyes. I think he's celebrating, letting me know that everything is all right. But then he swings the two fingers around to point at me: the international sign for *I'm watching you.* No one sees. It gives me shivers.

The pitcher's mound is squishy and the drizzle makes for a wet ball. When the ball is too wet to throw, I toss it to Coach Bill Karl, who stands at the edge of the diamond with a towel. As the wet one sails his way, he tosses a dry ball to me. We exchange balls this way through the first three innings.

The game starts badly, with a triple for the other team's first batter. Aside from a home run, what could be worse? I pitch so fast to the next batter, he doesn't even get up his nerve to swing. It's a perfect pitch, but the umpire calls a ball. I hear Phyllis in the stands ask, "Wha—?" Mom tells her, "Shhh."

The second pitch is even better than the first — right over the plate and just above the batter's knee. Jake, who is catcher, doesn't even have to move his glove to catch it. But the ump calls another ball. I look at Coach Bill Karl. He just gives me a fake smile and rolls his eyes.

I wind up, pitch again. Another perfect throw over the plate, a little low, the tiniest bit on the inside. The ump calls another ball. The crowd in the Home stands groan.

"Beautiful pitches, Allie," Phyllis yells. She's trying to make me feel better, but she's also, not so subtly, dissing the umpire.

I throw another fine pitch. Another ball is called. And the guy from Long Lake walks.

I look at Sal, who's in the stands with Mom and Phyllis. She shrugs, then circles her ear with a finger — *dingbat*. Coach Bill Karl fidgets. He calls time, starts walking toward the umpire, thinks better of it and approaches me instead. "Allie, try pitching a little higher. I don't know what's up with this Tim Tschida." I laugh at that. Tim Tschida is the Major League umpire said to have the smallest strike zone — the ball better be well above the knee and below the underarm if he's going to call *stirrrr-iiike*.

The next kid up is tall and as skinny as the baseball bat in his hands. His arms are so long he has to stand way to the back of the batting box to keep his swing over the plate. He nods his bony head at me. I wind up and pitch the fastest pitch I may ever have pitched. It's fuelled by my anger at the umpire and goes like a rocket. Jake doesn't move his glove at all for the ball to fly right into it. The skinny kid's mouth falls open in delayed shock.

And the ump calls a ball.

The skinny kid's thin lips stretch into a grin. Then he retracts the grin and nods again. Now I'm really angry. I wind up and pitch — right over the plate, right into Jake's glove, lots of pepper. I'm surprised the skinny kid's hat doesn't fly off his head.

The ball park is totally silent. Everyone watches the ump.

The ump turns his head and slowly looks at the crowd. He turns to nod sleepily at the batter, then at me. I smile. It's always smart to be on the umpire's good side. The ump starts to raise his right arm. But he isn't calling a strike. He grabs at his chest protector, claws with his fingers as if he's trying to get through it to his chest. Then he lifts a knee off the ground, spins a little on his other foot and falls to the mucky ground. You can actually hear the *splat*.

Everyone in the park starts shouting. The line ump, Coach Bill Karl and the other team's coach hurry toward the fallen man. They squat over him, talk to him, remove his mask. The rest of us do what we do whenever anyone is hurt during a game — we get down on one knee and wait. Mom and Phyllis run to the plate and clear people out of the way. They get to work, taking the man's pulse, removing his protective gear. In the middle of the activity, the umpire on the ground waves Coach Bill Karl over and whispers into his ear. Coach Bill Karl nods.

The ambulance drives right onto the diamond. The ambulance attendants confer with Phyllis and Mom, then lift the umpire onto a stretcher and into the ambulance. I feel very proud of my mom — of both of them . . . my moms.

Coach Bill Karl announces that the ump wanted the game to continue, that what he whispered into Coach Bill Karl's ear was "Play ball."

"Are there any umps in the stands who can take over?" Coach Bill Karl asks.

A Long Lake parent volunteers. She says she attended an umpire training camp in March and has since umped three mini-minor games. I can't stop staring as she straps on the shin guards, the chest protector and finally the helmet. She looks strange on the diamond.

Out of place. I know what it is: she's the first woman I've seen on the diamond all season, not counting Mom and Phyllis carrying my birthday cake to the mound or kneeling at the fallen umpire's side. All of the umpires and all of the coaches — even the girls' team coaches — are men. The one place there are women is in the score booth, pushing the buttons that light up on the big board. I've never even seen a man do that job. What's up with that?

The Long Lake volunteer takes position behind the batter and we're off. I strike out two players, one after the other, and we manage to hold the runner on third from coming in. The next batter gets a hit, though, a grounder that Francis nabs and makes to toss to first, but I scream at him, "Home!" He gets it in just as the runner slides in from third. The pinch umpire lifts her fist in the air with gusto and her voice is strong and sure. "Out!"

Francis glares at me for having told him what to do. But when someone yells, "Way to go, Francis!" his glare melts and he looks almost happy.

And for the first time in a week, I see him. I see Francis, rather than the bruise that I put on his cheek.

The top of the inning ends with no runs scored. Then it's the Wolverines at bat. I'm first, Eric second. I swing at the first pitch and hit a high foul over the fence.

"Heads!"

Bang. The ball lands on the Visitors dugout. I sure hope their ears are ringing. The little sisters and brothers in the stands run for the ball. Whoever gets to it first will hand it in at Concession for a bag of candy. Whoever thought that up was a genius! All foul balls get returned to the League.

A second pitch and I get a tip ball. That's strike two. Then another tip ball. Coach Bill Karl calls time and reminds me to swing a little sooner. I tell him that the pitcher is really good, that he's so fast I can't time my swings right. He just says, "Meet the ball, Allie." Another hit, another foul sailing high in the air, a total pop. I think it's going to land on the Visitors dugout again, but the Long Lake first baseman sprints and leaps, reaches high and wide and — amazingly — catches it. There's an explosion of laughter from the stands. Even the Home supporters are cheering such an amazing catch, the kind you wish you'd caught on camera and put up on the Web where it would get a million hits.

But I'm out. Eric takes a few wimpy warm-up swings, then steps up to the plate. No one cheers him, not even the boys in the dugout. I doubt his mom is even here.

"Go, Eric!" I shout from the dugout. Mine is the only voice in the park. Big Liam rolls his eyes and snickers. My face feels hot. I pray for someone else to cheer on Eric. Anyone!

"Like you can, Eric!" someone shouts from the

stands. I know that voice. It's Miles. He doesn't even know Eric. Why would he cheer for him? Maybe he's mocking me. That's probably it.

Cheering on Eric doesn't make a difference anyway. The pitcher doesn't pitch any of those eccentric high outside balls Eric likes so much, so Eric never gets a decent hit. He hits a foul that might have been a hit if the bat was dry. Then he gets the embarrassing kind of swinging strike, the kind you do when you're in mini-minors: he swings, misses, and spins, the weight of the bat pulling him around.

"Hey, 360-Eric," Big Liam yells.

The name catches on fast. "Way to go, 360-Eric," the boys say, high-fiving Eric when he returns to the dugout. Eric just smiles and laughs. He can laugh at himself, which is very cool. He loves baseball, but he doesn't have to be the winner.

The game is strange. No one can get a run. There are some decent hits, but tons of errors and lots of slow running. I think none of us can shake the memory of the umpire lying in the mud. After the sixth inning, the score is still 0–0. We play an extra inning but the score doesn't budge. Normally, we would keep playing until someone gets a run, but today, the coaches call Mr. Kelsiuk. The decision is to end the game, without a score, in honour of the umpire who was carried away in an ambulance.

I don't mind accepting a tie game, but the boys

grumble. They think it's stupid. They keep saying they just had to get one run in, and that they would have done it, too. It's like they're insulted, being asked to end the game on a tie. I don't know. I had a funny feeling that we could have played for hours with no one ever getting home. Like we were fated to play some strange, surreal ghost of a game, caring only about the play, with no interest in the score.

11 MAKING LEMONADE

"Have you noticed that the leaves have unfurled on the trees?" Phyllis asks at breakfast on Sunday. "And the baby swallows are crowding their nests? Have you noticed that the rain is warm when it falls? Have you noticed that it's full-on spring?"

"Yes, it's lovely, isn't it?" Mom says agreeably. "Yesterday, there were Popsicle wrappers on the sidewalk, and the woman in front of me at the pharmacy was buying suntan oil. I can't believe they still sell that stuff."

"Are you two nervous or something?" I ask.

"Yeah," Miles adds, pouring cereal into his bowl. "You're kind of over-chirpy."

"The decision comes out today," Phyllis reminds him.

"But that's not the only thing," Mom says.

"No, it isn't," Phyllis agrees. She clears her throat. "There's something we want to talk to you two about."

"What?" Miles asks.

"What is going on with Patches?" Phyllis asks.

"We found sardine tins in your rooms," Mom explains. "Lots of them."

"They're mostly in Miles's room," I say, anger boiling up. "He's the one feeding Patches, to win her over, to steal her."

"Yeah, well, I didn't tie up your favourite stuffy," Miles shouts.

"No, but you tied up my living cat!"

"I didn't want her jumping out the window."

"She is free to come and go."

"Is this true, Miles?" asks Mom. "You've been feeding sardines to Patches?"

"Yes," Miles mumbles.

"Why? We have lots of cat food for her. If you think we don't feed her well enough —"

"It's not that."

"What then?"

"I just wanted her —"

"Yeah! You wanted to steal her!" I yell.

"No, that's not true. I just like her. I wanted to make friends with her."

"She's MY cat."

"Okay, okay, you two." Mom reaches for her purse. "Listen, can you go to the store and get some juice? And the newspaper. It's got to be out by now."

"Go *together*?" I ask.

"Yes," Mom says firmly. "Together."

Walking down the street with stinky Miles is a nightmare. He breathes heavy and actually wipes his nose with his sleeve. We walk two blocks in silence, a raging silence.

"That Sal is a great hitter," he finally says. It's the last thing in the world I think I would hear from him.

"What's it to you?"

"I just mean that she's a good player. So is Annabel. And Sophia. They're all really strong."

"As strong as the boys?"

"It's different. I can't figure it out. They're super nice to me."

"Weird."

"I know you don't like me, Allie."

I suddenly feel bad that Miles thinks I don't like him. It's true that I don't like the way things have changed since our moms got together. I don't like the way Miles makes me feel like a stranger in my own house. But not liking Miles?

"That's not true," I say slowly.

"It isn't? It's not that I don't like you. I don't think I realized that Patches was *your* cat. I thought she just kind of wandered the house, you know? No one ever seems to spend much time with her."

"Hmph," I say. He's right. I know. I feel really bad about forgetting to play with Patches. I look at Miles. He's working his face weirdly, chewing his lips, squinting, blowing out his cheeks. He's thinking hard, I guess. Or trying not to cry.

"I think — well, the thing is — but I don't care — I just —" he stutters.

On a few of my trips into the city to meet with other two-mother families, they've held workshops where we kids are supposed to share our feelings about having two moms. I get a million thoughts at once and can only get bits of each to come out of my mouth. It looks like Miles is having the same problem. I can't watch any longer.

"Hey," I say. "How about getting a cat of your own? I know a place in Copper Bay. An animal shelter."

I almost tell him I'll go with him to Copper Bay, on the bus, but what am I thinking? That would require spending serious time together.

I push open the door to Gemma's Grocery. The air inside is cool. Mrs. Thompson is in the juice aisle. I haven't seen her since the last time I babysat Eli. I elbow Miles.
"I used to babysit her kids," I say quietly, nodding toward Mrs. Thompson. "But since our moms got together, she hasn't called once."

Miles nods knowingly. "Not everyone has an open mind," he says in a loud voice.

"Shh," I say. There's no way Mrs. Thompson can't have heard.

"Oh, it's true," Miles says, practically shouting. "Some people like to shut other people down. They want everyone to be as small as they are. That way they don't have to be afraid."

Mrs. Thompson stares at us. I pretend not to see her.

"Excuse me," Miles says, passing too closely to Mrs. Thompson. Mrs. Thompson hurries away.

"Miles, you shouldn't have done that!" I say.

"Why not? I'm sick and tired of people judging my mom — and your mom. I didn't like it either when they got together, but at least I had good reasons not to."

"Like what reasons?"

"What do you think?"

"I don't know."

"Unlike you, I had to leave my house. I had to leave my hometown. I had to leave my friends. I did have friends, you know."

Miles reaches for a bottle of lemonade.

"They said juice," I tell him.

"Well, this *is* juice. Lemon juice."

"Okay, but if we get in trouble, it's your fault."

"Wait a minute. You're agreeing to it. Do you want lemonade?"

"I just don't want to fight you."

"You fight with me all the time. Why not here?"

"Okay, okay." I feel tired all of a sudden. "I want lemonade."

Mom always says that if the world gives you lemons, make lemonade. Well, the world gave me Miles. Miles, who likes video games and hanging out in the dark; Miles, who tried to steal my cat from me. I never even thought that things had been hard on him, too. I realize that he and I have something really important in common — our moms loving each other openly in a small town where such a thing has never happened before.

"Hi, Miles," the cashier says when we get to the till. "Any bottles to return today?"

"No." Miles grits his teeth.

"Then no sardines to buy," the cashier says.

"No," Miles says again.

As the woman puts our lemonade and newspaper in a bag, Miles says, "The sardines were a mistake."

"Oh?" the cashier asks.

"He means he might get a cat of his own," I say.

"Oh," says the cashier, looking confused.

12 DOUBLE STANDARD

I take the bag and Miles follows me out of the store.

"Hey, Allie, I'm really sorry about Patches."

"You already said sorry," I say.

"No, I didn't. It's just that after six months in this town, I'm still a stranger. People look through me. You grew up here. It's your home. You know every person, every tree."

I stop and walk up to a tree.

"How are you, old friend," I say. "Let me introduce you to Miles. Miles, Elm. Elm, Miles."

"Pleased to meet you, Elm," Miles says.

We both smile. Imagine that! Smiling at the same time. Together.

Just then, Eric wheels toward us on his bike. When he sees us, he brakes so hard his bike skids. And my heart lurches.

"Eric!"

"That's 360-Eric to you," he corrects, grinning.

"I'm just introducing Miles around," I say. "Eric, Miles. Miles, Eric."

Eric's eyes go wide. "Miles? Miles the Mischief Maker?"

Miles shrugs. "I guess."

"What did the league decide?" Eric demands. "Do you get to play or not?"

"We forgot to check!"

Miles and I grab the newspaper from the grocery bag and spread it out on the grass.

"You made first page," Eric says, slapping Miles on the shoulder.

Little League Rules on Boy Who Wants to Play with Girls

The National Little League has ruled that a Juniper Bay boy cannot play on a local girls' team.

"It is simply against the rules," ruled National Little League President Tom Nanoo. "Girls need a safe and protected place to play ball. You have to see it this way: we are not so much forbidding a boy to play ball as we are protecting a girl's right to play ball in a supportive environment. Ever since we launched girls-only teams, the number of girls playing ball has increased tenfold. In fact, a hundredfold. We don't want to lose that."

Miles Kowalchuk asked to play on the girls' team at the start of the baseball season. He attends girls' practices but watches games from the dugout.

The Juniper Bay Times received this news at deadline; it

has not yet been able to reach Miles for comment. It is not known whether he will continue to attend practices.

"I can't believe it," Miles moans.

"I don't get it," Eric says. "The girls don't mind, do they?"

"No," says Miles. "The girls want me to play."

"A 'safe and protected' environment?" I say. "Do they think we're helpless weaklings?"

"That's not what they said," Eric says. "Really, they're saying they want girls to play ball. And that girls won't unless there are teams especially for them. It's kind of like, if you were in Grade 8 and the track team is all Grade 7s, are you going to want to join?

"I told my mom about you, Miles, and we've been reading up about the game. Girls weren't allowed into the Little League of America until 1974! In the 1950s, a girl dressed up as a boy and tried out. They found out she was a girl once she made the cut, and they let her stay, because it was a novelty."

"That's what I hoped Island League would do," Miles says. "Let me stay, just this once, at least."

"An eleven-year old girl — Jenny Fulle — took Little League to court in 1974 and not only did they let her in, they created a whole softball program that girls could sign up for."

"So a girl once did what you're trying to do," I say, looking at Miles.

"But there's a difference," Eric says. "Miles is already allowed to play ball."

"But I have to play with the boys!"

Eric and I laugh.

"I might have started out because I was nervous about Allie playing on my team. I was worried she'd tease me, or be hard on me," Miles says. He shrugs and looks sheepish. I feel my face grow hot. Have I really been hard on *him*? Maybe I have been. Miles continues. "But now I really don't want to keep playing on the boys' team. It's such a drag. They're always pushing each other, and they're so serious all the time, strutting around. Some of them even spit as if they're in the big leagues. It's gross!"

I think of all the girls who play ball in Juniper Bay. Playing with Annabel and Sal and Hannah and Sophia made me who I am. Our team photos are on my dresser. Every year, we get bigger and more sure in those photos. We *grow*. If we'd had to play with boys all those years, I doubt we'd still be playing ball.

"I know what that's like," I say. "All that strutting around. But it's like you're trying to undo what that girl — Jenny Fulle — did in 1974."

"That's not true —" Miles says.

"Yes, it is."

Up until now, I've been annoyed by Miles. But maybe I hated the *idea* of him without thinking about him as a person. He was a jerk sometimes, sure, but my behaviour was knee-jerk. He was a stranger shoved into my house, my life, and I had to push back. But Sal likes Miles, and she's right about him. I think about how he handled Mrs. Thompson in the grocery store and how he talked about feeling lonely and how he didn't realize that Patches was mine. Maybe the kid is okay after all.

But now it feels like we've got something real to fight about. Something important. I'm afraid that if Miles got into the Angels, my memories of playing ball with all my friends would be infected, rained on, as if they never were as sunny as they felt. It's not like I'm fighting against him, though; it's more like I'm fighting to protect years of memories.

"I support you, dude," Eric is telling Miles. "You should be able to play with whoever you want."

"Thanks," Miles says.

Miles and Eric both look at me.

"I respect what you're doing, Miles," I say. "But I don't agree with it."

I get excited when I think of Jenny Fulle in 1974 pushing for a place in the little league. I feel proud. I'm kind of excited by what Miles is doing, too. I want to feel proud of him, but it doesn't feel like he's opening new ground. It feels like he's invading my world — again. It puts me on guard.

"Hey! Check this out!" Eric points to another headline in the paper.

Umpire Has Heart Attack On The Diamond

Little League Umpire Wayne Mitchell made erratic calls during the boys' majors game Friday night before falling to the ground from a minor heart attack. Mitchell was taken to hospital and kept overnight for observation. He is expected to make a full recovery.

Mitchell had called several balls on pitches that were obviously strikes, thrown by Allie Jenkinson. Her presence on the boys' team is said to have sparked Miles Kowalchuk's bid to be on the girls' team, the Angels. According to one source, the two are nemeses.

Before being driven off the diamond in an ambulance, Mitchell gave his blessing for the game to continue. But after nine innings plus an extra tenth, both teams decided to end the game with a 0–0 score in Mitchell's honour.

"When someone's life is on the line, it isn't the time to think about the score," long-time Coach Bill Karl explained. "It's a time for hope. For community over competition."

In an interview at his home, Mitchell said he was honoured by the gesture. "If you think about it, life is a ball game," he said cryptically, before dozing off. This *Juniper Bay Times* reporter covered him with a blanket and quietly left.

"Well, I'm glad he's going to be okay," I say.

"So, you two are nemeses, eh?" Eric says. "You don't look like nemeses."

I edge away from Miles. "Oh, we are."

"But that's not why I —" Miles starts to say.

"How do you even know each other?" Eric asks.

"It's a long story," I say.

"We're siblings," Miles says.

I stare at him in disbelief.

"Forced siblings," Miles corrects himself. "Our — uh, parents fell in love and we have to go along with it."

I notice Miles doesn't say "our mothers." I've done the same thing, said "parents" when I might have said "moms." The only place I freely refer to having "moms" is at the group we go to in the big city.

"So, like, your mom and dad moved in with each other and you had to go along with it?"

"Yep," Miles and I say flatly, both of us half-lying.

"Whose dad and whose mom?" Eric is asking.

"My mom," I say quickly.

"So, Miles's dad."

"We better get back," Miles says.

Miles and I walk home in silence. I'm thinking about how much fun we had in the grocery store, and about Eric, and about Miles's campaign, and about being on the Wolverines. I'm playing so hard. It isn't just that I want to prove myself to the boys, there's an atmosphere on the boys' team, a feeling that you can go far. And, of course, the possibility is there. The boys can go all the way to major leagues. They strut around like MLB players. Like they're just working their way up.

The girls — well, some of us talk about playing college ball, but it stops there.

Mom and Phyllis don't care that we got lemonade. I think they're just glad that Miles and I spent time together. They jump on the newspaper and then freak out. Phyllis thinks Miles should be able to do whatever he wants to do. Mom tries to soothe her. But I notice that she doesn't put down the League the way Phyllis does. She just listens and nods.

13 HAPPY THE WAY THINGS ARE

Mom, Phyllis, Miles, and I are having supper in the dining room. We're eating some barley, black bean, and cheese concoction Phyllis made that isn't all bad, actually, as long as you pile on the ketchup. It's still light out.

"Summer solstice is around the corner," Mom says. "The longest day of the year."

Someone knocks at the back door.

"That's the first time anyone's come to the back door since we moved in," Phyllis says. "Who's sneaking around?"

She opens the door.

"Mayor Sorenson! What's up?"

"It's your boy. I got a call from the newspaper in the big city. They're asking me what's going on here. They want to know why a boy needs to play on a girls' team so badly. I couldn't answer, Ma'am. I don't know of one good reason."

"I see."

"Can you get him to change his mind?"

"I don't think so," Phyllis says. "His mind is his own."

"The Island Little League ruled that he cannot play on the girls' team. Isn't that enough?"

"The girls don't mind him being on the team."

"But where does it end? We can't have boys wanting to be on girls' teams. A boy needs to be a boy."

Miles gets up from the table and joins his mom at the back door.

"I'm still a boy," he says. "I'll always be a boy no matter what I do."

"I mean a normal boy," Mayor Sorenson stutters.

Suddenly, something clicks inside me. Mayor Sorenson is calling my family abnormal, and months of being seen as a freak bring me to my feet.

"What about me?" I ask, joining everyone. "I play with the boys and no one has a problem with that. They don't say I'm an abnormal girl."

"Well, that's because you're good. You're a strong player. You put the game first. It doesn't matter that you're a girl."

"Yes, it does," I say, anger rising in me. "It matters every pitch I throw that I'm a girl. It matters every runner I bat in. Every steal I make. Every second I'm on the diamond, I'm a girl, and it matters."

"My son will do what he believes is the right thing," Phyllis says, her voice clipped. "Right now, that is to see if there isn't a place where he's truly comfortable."

I look at Miles. Is that true? Is he just looking for

somewhere that feels comfortable? I think of how rough it's been for me on the Wolverines, how the boys are mean to each other and never sing, how they hold back their tears and act so brave.

"I meant to cause a little trouble, but I didn't mean to cause this much," Miles says. "I'm responsible for a little of it. But I'm not responsible for all of it."

"That's right," Phyllis says.

My mom joins us and puts her arm around Phyllis's shoulder. Phyllis reaches up and squeezes Mom's hand. And I get it. They have also had to pick a fight simply to be who they are. They have had to upset a whole lot of people just to make room for the two of them. But there's a difference — they didn't displace anyone. They just added themselves. If Miles gets onto the girls' team, would a place for a girl be lost? Would she head over to the empty spot made on a boys' team? I doubt it.

I'm not sure what to think, but Mom has said that family comes first, no matter what. I might disagree with Miles, but I've got to support him.

"He's making people think," I say. "That's not a bad thing."

Mayor Sorenson looks at us. We each return his angry stare with a blank smile. Finally, he shakes his head and reaches behind him for the door handle.

"I don't understand you people," he says, backing out of our kitchen. "Why can't you just be happy the way things are?"

★★★

We thought we'd beat Fisher Branch hands down, but the score stays even for the first three innings. It's the top of the fourth inning and the Wolverines are at bat.

I made a Get Well Soon card to pass around in the dugout, with a weaving of ribbon in our team colours I made glued to the front. I'll bike it over to the umpire's house once everyone has signed it. I quietly hand it to one of the boys, but no one touches it. It just floats around on the bench, then starts to get trampled on the ground.

Coach Bill Karl puts his head into the dugout. "What's that?"

"Something stupid," Big Liam answers.

"Whose is it?"

"Hers," Big Liam says, jerking his thumb toward me.

"Get it out of the dugout," Coach Bill Karl says.

"It's a card for the umpire," I say.

"I can't hear you."

"It's a Get Well card for the umpire who had the heart attack."

"Well, what's it doing in here?"

"I thought everyone could sign it."

"And you call it stupid?" Coach Bill Karl asks Big Liam.

"I didn't know what it was," Big Liam says.

"Neither did I," Eric says, putting his hand out. "I'll sign it."

"Yeah," Francis says.

"Cool," Big Liam adds.

"Allie, can I talk to you for a minute?" Coach Bill Karl says.

I head out of the dugout.

"Allie," Coach Bill Karl says. "I know that the boys haven't given you the easiest time. They haven't welcomed you with open arms."

"That's for sure," I say.

"But, you know what, Allie? You haven't made it easy either."

"What? I've kept to myself, I — "

"That's just the problem. You're all quiet and hiding. You're not being Allie. How can they buddy up to you if you don't show them who you are?"

"*I'm* causing the problem?"

"No. You're causing *some* of it. Fix your little bit and then maybe they can fix their part. Now get out there. You're at bat. And don't swing at the first pitch. They're starting a new pitcher. Get to know his speed."

I hurriedly take a few practice swings and hustle into the batting box.

"Go, Allie!" Mom yells from the stands.

"Like you can!" Phyllis adds.

"Woot!" Miles puts in.

The pitcher adjusts his cap, spits to the side of the mound, grinds a foot into the dirt like a bull about to charge, winds up and sends the ball toward me.

It's a perfect pitch, going slow-mo and everything, and the sweet spot on my bat is humming. I'm torn between Coach Bill Karl's advice not to swing at the first pitch and this beautiful, deliciously excellent throw.

I can't commit to the swing — but it's too late to pull back. I get a lame hit, barely more than a bunt that rolls straight to the pitcher.

"Ohhh," the crowd groans.

"Run!" Phyllis screams.

"Run, Allie!" Eric yells. "Pump those legs."

I do what I can. And I'm very lucky because the pitcher's throw is off. The first baseman has to take his foot off the bag to get it, which is when I stomp in. I pump my legs like Eric said. I'm safe on the bag, panting, my stomach hurting from running so hard, when Big Liam takes the bat.

The pitcher winds up and throws. I'm nearly halfway between first and second when I hear the crack of Big Liam's bat. Then — *whompf* — I'm on the ground, agony charging through my side. Coach Bill Karl hustles over while Big Liam looks on from first. I'm rolling on the ground, trying to rub out the pain.

I'm out, I know that. That's the rule. You get hit by the ball when you're not on base and you're out. Coach Bill Karl helps me hobble off the field. The other players are down on a knee. When I pass first base, Big Liam asks, "You okay?"

"My fault for not watching the ball," I say, trying to suck in my tears.

"It's still got to hurt, your fault or not."

"It does," I say, letting my tears fall. "It does."

"Sorry."

"That's all right." I say, looking at him through the blur of my tears. For the first time all season, Big Liam smiles at me.

Once the pain eases, Coach Bill Karl sits next to me on the bench.

"Why did you bat? I asked you not to."

"It was such a perfect pitch. It was in just the right spot."

"Then why was your hit so poor?"

"Because I was trying to hold back. I was confused. Conflicting messages."

"Mine comes first."

"But that pitch, Coach Bill Karl — really!"

"Hm," Coach Bill Karl grunts. "Sent by the baseball gods, huh?"

"Or goddesses," I say.

"There's my Allie."

Fisher Branch must have used up all its steam holding us off for those early innings, because we get eight runs in the fourth inning despite my early out. Fisher Branch has error after error, over-throws and missed catches.

Eric actually gets a decent hit and over-runs first

base by about six metres. He just picked up a whole lot of steam, I guess. And when he gets back to the bag, he spins on it, the guys in the dugout chanting, "360-Eric, 360-Eric!" From then on, Eric spins every time he lands a base.

The game ends with a score of 12–8 for the Wolverines. In the middle of the celebration, Albert of the Big Ears hands me the Get Well card. "I made sure everyone signed it," he says.

"Right," I say, trying to act cool. Then I remember Coach Bill Karl's pep talk about being myself. "That's really, really awesome."

Eric and I help Bill Karl put away the bases and chalk markers, and lock up the shed. The guy who runs the concession gives us a couple of hamburgers for free. They're cold, but tasty enough. While we sit in the empty stands eating, Eric points to the woods beside the park.

"Want to go blue-grey taildropper slug spotting?" he asks.

"I'm dying to go blue-grey taildropper slug spotting," I deadpan.

Actually, hunting for slugs sounds weirdly exciting. When Mom and Phyllis were first together, Phyllis drove all the way into town just to go with Mom to the dump. "When you're in love," Mom told me. "Everything is wonderful, even a trip to a stinking garbage heap." I'm not saying I'm in love with Eric, just interested in spending time with him. I remember what Coach Bill Karl said, about not being afraid to be a girl. So I say a little more.

"For some reason, that sounds like fun. It would be cool to hang out with you some more, too."

Eric smiles his magic slanted smile. Then he reaches for my visor and swivels my ball cap around.

"Why did you do that?" I say.

Eric shrugs. "So I can see your face. Your whole face."

"Well, to be fair, you have to turn your hat around, too," I say.

"Technically, if it's going to be even, *you* have to turn my hat around."

"Okay."

I swivel 360-Eric's cap around 180 degrees. Then we just sit there, chewing the last bites of our cold hamburgers.

14 BEING MYSELF

I've never seen a blue-grey taildropper, but Eric pulls a creased pamphlet out of his baseball bag. The slug we're looking for is a solid colour, either a misty grey or a cornflower blue or some shade in between. In spring, it's no bigger than the tip of my pinkie finger. It's gross-looking of course, slimy and shaped like a thick worm. But it has a sort of humbleness about it. It's smart in design, too — unlike other slugs, it "drops" its tail if a predator gets hold of it. You can see a line right across its body where its tail will come off if needed. That would be handy in baseball if you could just shake off any part of you that gets tagged and keep on running.

Once we're in the woods, Eric points out oak trees, big leaf maple trees, oceanspray bushes, leaf litter and mushrooms — places that the taildropper is comfortable. Then we get to it, crouching and creeping, peering and squinting. We think *Yes! Got one!* then feel stupid and disappointed when the "slug" turns out to be the fallen petal of a flower or, in one case, a piece of yarn that I snag for a future weaving. I grab a bunch of grasses and pine needles, too.

After an hour, Eric and I take a break. "I *know* there are taildroppers in these woods," Eric says. "There have to be."

A crow gurgles in the branches above us. Mice and voles skitter in the underbrush. A squirrel spirals up the trunk of a large oak. I climb a tree, too; my hands and baseball uniform get sticky with spruce sap. There's a good view from the top. I see our town, our dull little town, filled with people running errands, the downtown offices and shops ringed by houses, the whole town pressed against the curves of Juniper Bay, where fishing boats bob on the grey-blue water. I spy the town graveyard in the distance, where farmland begins. Dad and I used to bike that way to the U-Picks for strawberries and blueberries in the spring.

"Let's go for a ride," I say.

Eric leaps up. "Great idea."

The town is noisy as we bike through. Eric and I don't talk much. Then we reach the country again and it's like we've broken the sound barrier. Total silence. Well, not really — birds sing and caw and the last leaves on the trees rustle in the breeze. But there's no urgency, no being busy. That's a kind of quiet. As we pedal up the lane to the graveyard, the gravel stones crunch under our tires.

We lean our bikes against a wall, then wander

between the gravestones, reading out the strange old names — Ezekial, Archibald, Thaddeus. Henrietta, Temperance, Winifred. Often, under the men's names the jobs they did are carved into the stone: Shipwright, Captain in the British Navy, Doctor. But under the women's names, there aren't any professions, only connections: Wife Of, Daughter Of, Mother Of. We come upon the Mayors Grove, where the town's past mayors are buried: John McIntosh, Uriah Kettle, Ian Barrist, Peter Langley, Stanley Boyersmith.

"One day, Mayor Sorenson will lie here," I say.

"That sounds like a threat," Eric says, laughing.

We're making our way out of the cemetery when I pass a plain grave with two angels carved into it. I know the name instantly: *Olivia Karl 1934–2009*. I squat before it, run my finger along the smooth grooves of its letters.

"Stay here," I tell Eric, standing up.

I start to circle Olivia Karl's gravestone, making a wider and wider path around it until other headstones are inside my orbit. I read every name on those headstones. Finally, I find a gravestone identical to Olivia Karl's — simple, with the same carving of two angels together holding a heart. It says *Mandy Hartley 1936–2009*. It's twenty feet from Olivia's.

"I know something about these women," I say.

But Eric doesn't hear me. I repeat, "I know something!"

"What?" he asks.

I'm not sure that I should tell, whether or not I should break the quiet air with this secret that has been kept in our town for more than forty years. But surely Olivia and Mandy are safe now.

"Well, they were baseball players when they were our age," I begin safely. "In the Little League. Later, they became girlfriend and girlfriend. But they couldn't tell anyone. They were too afraid. They lived together for forty years, pretending they were cousins. Hardly anyone knows the truth."

"How do you know?"

"Coach Bill Karl told me. I don't know if he's told anyone else, so you better keep it a secret."

"But why did he tell *you?*"

I don't know how to answer him. I've told other kids about Mom and Phyllis, but telling Eric is harder. I didn't care if the other kids rejected me. But with Eric, I care very much about what he thinks.

"It's okay," he says. "I don't mean to be nosy."

"The thing is, my mom lives with Miles's *mom*, not his dad."

"Oh," Eric says. He looks stunned, even a little horrified. "And people know?"

"People know," I say.

"Oh, wow."

He just stands there. I wait in dread. If he rejects Mom and Phyllis, it's like he rejects me, too.

Then he looks at me. "Are you . . . a lesbian, too?"

"No! That isn't how it works!"

"I know, I know. That was stupid of me. It's just it would suck — for me — if you were."

"Because then you couldn't be my friend?" I feel my blood warm, anger mounting.

"No, no, that's not it. Because . . . because then I couldn't be more than your friend."

I stand there looking at him like he's nuts. What is he talking about?

Oh!

"Oh," I say.

Eric looks at his feet. I look at mine.

"But as for Olivia and Mandy, yeah, that sucks," he says. "If you couldn't tell anyone who you really were. Like it was a crime or something."

"Yep. It would suck," I say, relieved that he's on board.

"Can we get their graves closer to each other?" Eric asks.

"They're pretty heavy." I laugh.

"I have an idea," Eric says. He gets a baseball from his sports bag. "Let's play catch."

So that's what we do. I stand at Mandy's grave and Eric stands at Olivia's and we throw the ball back and forth. From Mandy's grave to Olivia's grave, from Olivia to Mandy. It feels like we're tying the graves together with the strands of our throws. I imagine the paths of our throws passing under and over each other, weaving together, until all that distance between their graves is braided together. Woven taut.

15 PLAYING LIKE LITTLE KIDS

- coach thor says he has to respect the League ruling

- so Miles is out?

- looks that way. and we all want him to stay. he's nice. cute too.

- Sal!

- how is he doing

- miserable. he's in the dark in his room. he didn't even come out for supper. he wants to play ball but now all the teams are full

- why don't you give him your spot on the Wolverines

- no

- I thought you didn't like it

- I'm still learning stuff

- want to play catch?

- sure. see you at the park in ten.

Miles's room is dark and stuffy. The curtains are closed. The only light is from the video game he's playing. It makes his face look bruised.

"Knock-knock," I say.

"Yeah?"

Miles doesn't take his eyes off the screen.

"Just brought someone to see you," I say.

I let Patches out of my arms. She runs straight for the dresser and sniffs at the bottom drawer.

"There's nothing in there," Miles tells her flatly, not even turning to look at her.

The newspaper article with the Island Little League ruling is on the bulletin board above his desk, shot through with darts, staples, a ballpoint pen and a couple of butter knives.

"Wow," I say.

Miles smirks. "Yeah. That was fun. For a moment."

"Not too happy, eh?"

"What do you think?"

"Hey, want to come play catch with me and Sal at the park?"

"No."

Patches tries heading out the door. I don't let Miles see me block her with my leg and push her back into his room.

"Okay," I say, closing the door behind me tightly, so Patches has to stay with him. If anyone needs company right now, it's Miles. I grab my glove, jump on my bike and head over to the park.

It's a beautiful summer evening. The day's heat still hangs in the air. I feel really awake; restless. Sal's already at the park with Annabel and Sophia. Sal and I play catch while the other two climb a tree and watch us from above. After a while, Annabel texts Hannah and Courtney to come with extra gloves and a baseball bat. Courtney texts back that she has two cousins in town, and could they play, too? After we say yes, she tells us, "They're boys." That makes us giddy.

Jake and Albert bike into the park. When they hear our plans to get a game going, they head home to get their baseball gloves. Hazel and Sienna get the news and show up, too. Lots of kids show up, even some of the girls on other girls' teams. And finally Eric. Sal makes fun of me for smiling like crazy when he shows up. But Eric's smile is big, too. Courtney arrives with her cousins, who aren't as good-looking as Eric, but nice enough. Pretty soon, we've got enough players for a game. Eric is named the captain of one team, Sal the other. They put their hands on the fat end of a baseball bat and work their way up, one hand above the other, until Eric is able to stretch out his long thumb and tap the top of the bat. He gets to choose first. He chooses me.

"Hey!" Sal says. "I wanted her."

Something catches her eye across the park. Her jaw drops. Mine, too. Who do we see dawdling up the park path but Miles. Miles! I expect him to be shrouded in darkness, to be carrying that shell of his closed-up bedroom with him, but he looks bright. He even looks hopeful. He's got a glove in one hand.

"What changed your mind?" I ask when he's closer.

"Patches went out my window," he says. "So, I went out the window, too."

We grin at each other.

"You're on *my* team," Sal tells him, pulling him by the arm.

Our team is at bat first. Hannah pitches. I feel a stab of homesickness watching her. I've hardly seen her all season. She's had her hair cut, and her pitching rocks, her throws even faster than last year. She throws two beautiful pitches, swinging strikes. Then the batter — one of Courtney's cousins from California — hits four foul balls in a row, the ball going everywhere except where it should. Poor Hannah. I hate third fouls. All that work and you get nothing. Hannah looks at first base, then back at third, as if by this slow shake of her head, she can clear out her frustration. Courtney's cousin gets a hit. A big one. Right into right outfield. He makes it to second.

Courtney's up to bat next. She hits a double on the first pitch and her cousin makes it home. Then I'm up. I swing twice. Hannah is fast. I'll just have to swing a little sooner. I do. I get a huge hit — right into the outfield. Right into Miles's glove. Out!

I shake my head. I should be annoyed, but I'm laughing. Why? Because I'm tired of competing with Miles. I'm just glad, too, that he's out of that stinky room. Somehow I feel as cooped up as he is when he's there. I feel the gloom and his sadness. I feel like they're my fault somehow. Maybe I want him to be happy because then I can be happy. Is that it? It's selfish, but maybe it's the best I can do for now.

Eric's up next. He gets three balls, two strikes — one of those super full counts I like — and then he gets a cracking hit. His legs are a blur as he runs. He's well past second by the time Courtney makes it into home. But the ball arrives at third, so he has to back up. The next two batters get out at first, while Eric manages to steal home.

Then Sal's team is at bat. I get to pitch. Sal bats first. I kind of want her to get a great hit, because she's my friend. But mostly I want to strike her out. I stick my tongue out at her. She sticks her tongue out at me. I'm a little scared — she's an awesome hitter. She does her trademark moves. She takes three practice swings, grinds her heels into the dirt, squats down with her right knee turned slightly in, raises her index fingers to check that they're aligned on the bat, and then looks my way.

I throw so hard I grunt. She swings and misses. I throw again, and she bunts! My catcher — Jake — grabs the ball and throws, hoping to get her out at first, but the ball hits Sal hard on the back. Poor Sal! She falls to the ground sobbing.

A bunch of us hurry over to help her. But Jake stays at the plate, yelling "She broke her line! She broke her line!"

"Yeah, and you nearly broke her back," Annabel shouts at him.

Sal knows she should be out and is willing to accept her fate, but she shows us why she broke her line. She was avoiding a hole on the baseline — she didn't want to sprain her ankle. Miles immediately fills it in with dirt. Meanwhile, Eric talks to Jake. He speaks calmly and Jake seems to listen to what he's saying.

After a while, Jake approaches Sal and says, "Hey, are you okay? Uh, sorry. I should have helped you up."

Sal says, "That's okay," and hobbles to the dugout. We debate what should happen. Some of us think she should be able to take first as compensation — it's not her fault there was a hole — but Sal insists on playing by the rules. We compromise. Next inning, she'll be first at bat.

Miles is up next. The kids cheer him on. If he hadn't gotten me out, I would be easy on him. I send a fast one, slightly inside.

Strike.

I pitch again. Ball. Then another ball. And another one. I would have called it a strike, but most of the kids say it was a ball. That's how we're umping — if there's a disagreement, we try to get everyone to agree, or have a vote with majority ruling. I'm off my game. *Focusfocusfocus.*

Strike.

Full count. Time for that old time-warp special. But

just as I let go of the ball, Sal yells, "Watch out for her changeup!"

Aw, Sal!

Miles slows his swing and gets a wicked hit, way into outfield. He is smiling — beaming — as he runs the bases. The kids are going crazy, jumping up and down, yelling at the outfielder, one of Courtney's cousins. "Hurry it up, whatever your name is," Sienna calls at one point. Miles slides into home just before the ball. His teammates surround him, jumping up and down. I give Sal a dirty look but then we both look at Miles, who is in his glory. He's actually laughing. I shrug. Let him have it. It turns out to be the only homerun of the game.

The air cools and the mosquitoes start biting, but we play for hours. At one point Big Liam comes through on his bike and watches for a while, his arms crossed. Eric invites him to join in, but he just smirks, as if we're idiots, as if we're little kids. I watch him as he pedals off: there's something familiar about him. The weight in his shoulders, the way he holds his head stiffly. Loneliness. That's what it is. The same look that Miles used to wear. I look at Miles. He and Sal are laughing together on the bench and she's showing him how she lines up her hands on the bat. He's so relaxed, so light, so open I hardly recognize him. He's happy.

We all are. It feels as though Juniper Bay belongs to us. And to the crickets in the grass and the crows overhead and even the taildropper slugs, wherever they are. Finally, we tire out. We sit in the stands, telling stories, teasing each other. Eric and I lean against each other, and it's great. It's getting dark when people's ringtones start to go off: our parents calling us home. I know Miles is bummed about not winning his fight. But I also know that girls need their baseball teams.

16 TRIPLE PLAY

"Why don't you give me your spot on the Wolverines? And go back to the Angels?" Miles asks me.

"That could work," Sal says.

"No way. I'm happy with the Wolverines, for now, anyway. It was your choice to challenge things," I remind Miles.

"Yeah, I know. I have to take my lumps."

"You were brave," Phyllis says, slowing the car as we arrive at Copper Bay. "I never knew there was activist in you."

"Oh, I did. I've seen him get the last bowl of cereal for himself," I say. "But really, he just did it to meet girls."

"That's not true!" Miles says. "Not the way you're suggesting. But it's true, I like girls. I like how you talk together and how you play ball. You perfect the plays and you work as a team. Boys baseball gets nutty. Everyone starts acting like they're going to make it into the big leagues. Even the coaches start acting that way, pushing you. The strongest players act all macho."

"You've never been one to swagger," Phyllis says.

"We don't have major leagues to make it into," Sal says. "To dream about. I sure wish we did. Women in basketball got the WNBA."

"Last year, in Cedar Grove, where we used to live, the girls' team made it to the provincials," Miles says. "There are two ballparks in Cedar Grove. One is fancy new and the other is old and crumbling. The girls practised in the fancy new park. But then the boys' team qualified for the provincials, too, and the girls got bumped from the fancy park to the crumbling one. The boys got the nice park because they have a 'real future' in the sport. I didn't want to be part of that. It's too . . . boasty."

"Why can't you work to change the boys' team? You know, show them how to be more like a team, and less macho," I say. "Get them singing!"

"They won't listen to me," Miles says.

"You got the whole town listening to you," Sal says. "From now on, people will think twice when there's a no-boys or no-girls rule."

"There it is! The Copper Bay Cat Rescue," I say. "Stop the car."

I told our moms at breakfast that Miles wanted a kitten. So here we are. We enter the old brick building and are led into a room with a dozen cats — old ones in beds, some at scratching posts, kittens wrestling. Signs on the wall encourage the adoption of black cats.

"People don't want them. They think they're bad luck," the vet tells us. "Superstition."

"Just because they're black?" Miles asks. "That's crazy. That is *stupid*stition."

So Miles the Fair-Minded chooses a black kitten. He calls her Triple. We talked him out of calling her Homer — too much like homely, Mom argued. Miles baby talks to Triple all the way home.

"You'll make a good pet owner," I tell him.

"Thanks," he says. "Just like I make a decent mom's girlfriend's son?"

"I guess," I say.

"Aww," Sal pipes in.

But she isn't commenting about me and Miles. She's gazing at Triple, who is cleaning her furry little black toes with her tiny pink tongue.

"She's the cutest cat in the whole world," Sal says.

"Not including Patches," I say.

But Miles and Sal are too busy cooing at Triple together to hear me.

So I guess Patches is my cat again. I'm trying to be good to her. I spend part of my allowance each week on sardines. She likes the ones in spring water best.

After watching Hannah pitch so well, and hearing Kate and Sienna chanting the season's new rhymes in the dugout, I've decided to go back to the Angels next season. It's not that I'm not good enough to play with the boys. Maybe it's that, since none of them think like Miles, they're not good enough to play with me.

Still, it's gotten better on the Wolverines. Albert and Jake have warmed up to me, now that I'm being more myself. And I've accepted that Big Liam will never be on my side. The rest cheer me on at bat. They call me Al, though, which irks me.

It also irks me that Coach Bill Karl calls me first base*man* when I play that position. And how about those states*men* Miles said he had to give in to? The mayor, the president of the Little League, the coaches, all of the umps minus that one who volunteered after the heart attack — all of them are men. All of them are grown-up boys. And all those dead mayors in Mayors Grove — them, too. And all those men in the graveyard who got to be more than someone's spouse or parent.

I don't know what to do about all the men making the decisions, running the show, though I know they think they were just protecting a girl's right to play baseball. Mom suspects it's mostly because they don't want a boy confusing things by playing with the girls, but I'm glad I have a place on a girls team like the Angels. And it's okay to be irked. That's what Miles taught me. Even when it felt like every adult in town was against him, he stayed sure, he stayed grumpy. It's what the moms taught me too: if there isn't any trouble, there won't be any change for the better.

Did I get my birthday wish? Did I pitch a shutout

game this year? There was that 0–0 game the day the umpire fell down into the trampled mud at home plate. But both teams pitched a shutout then. And knowing, as we swung, that an umpire was in an ambulance, being rushed down a bright hallway into an operating room, the victory wasn't so sweet. Next year, though, I'll do it.

Unusual Number of Baseball Injuries in Region

An unusual number of baseball-related injuries have been recorded this year in the region, including a scratched cornea, badly bruised cheek, fat lip, a swollen leg and a bruised back. And let's not forget that heart attack sustained by umpire Wayne Mitchell.

"Well, it hasn't been a boring season, I'll say that," noted Little League President Tom Kelsiuk. "I don't know why we've had so many injuries. Perhaps someone on high just wanted a little more action."

Coach Thor Danielson shrugged when asked to comment. "Look, getting hit by a ball is an inherent part of the game. You've got to take your lumps, you know?"

Blue-Grey Taildropper Slugs Identified in Juniper Bay

Two middle-school students, Allie Jenkinson and Eric Magnus, discovered six blue-grey taildropper slugs in the woods beside the Memorial Ball Diamond, creating a wave of excitement about the future of the species.

"It's astonishing news," said Eric's mother, Julie Magnus, a scientist researching the tiny endangered slug. "It's all we've hoped for."

Allie and Eric regularly look for the slug, a species on the verge of extinction.

"Looking for them is addictive," Allie said. "It's quiet and private and hopeful."

The two students have formally requested that the Mayor declare the woods protected habitat.

"We'd also like to see the forest formally named," Allie said. "Perhaps after Ida Frond, the first woman to practice medicine in Juniper Bay."

Allie and Eric say they will continue to look for slugs.

"Hanging out with Allie is addictive," said Eric. "She's smart and energetic and lots of fun."

Weddings in Juniper Bay

Allie Jenkinson and Miles Kowalchuk are pleased to announce the marriage of their mothers, Phyllis Kowalchuk and Suzanne Herring. The wedding between the two "head nurses" will take place on August 15 at City Hall. The two women made local history recently by starting an umpire training school for girls and women.

ACKNOWLEDGMENTS

This book was written for the 2012 Beacon Hill Little League Major Girls Provincial Champions — strong, determined, and graceful, every one: Hazel, Salma, Hannah, Kate, Sienna, Emma, Kaia, Analyn, Amelia, Molly, Haleisha and Courtney. Never give up your power!

This book is also for Jenny Fulle. And for all boys. Be who you are.

Thanks, too, to Karl, Thor, Deb, Mallory, and Kelsey. And especially to Bill Hawkins, who champions girls in ball in countless ways.

Thank you, too, to Ezra, my first reader; Catherine Shields, my first editor; Alden; Max; Sophia; and Scott.